THE COCKFIGHTER

The Cockfighter

A NOVEL BY FRANK MANLEY

ANCHOR BOOKS

DOUBLEDAY

NEW YORK   LONDON   TORONTO   SYDNEY   AUCKLAND

AN ANCHOR BOOK
PUBLISHED BY DOUBLEDAY
a division of Random House, Inc.
1540 Broadway, New York, New York 10036

ANCHOR BOOKS, DOUBLEDAY, and the portrayal of an anchor are
trademarks of Doubleday, a division of Random House, Inc.

The Cockfighter was originally published in hardcover by Coffee House Press
in 1998. The Anchor Books edition is published by arrangement
with Coffee House Press.

Book design by Kelly N. Kofron
Cover photograph © Hal Herzog, "Young Cockfighter"

AUTHOR ACKNOWLEDGMENT
I wish to thank the National Endowment for the Arts, that great
beleaguered institution, for a Creative Writing Fellowship in Fiction
that enabled me to write this book.

Library of Congress Cataloging-in-Publication Data

Manley, Frank.
    The cockfighter : a novel by Frank Manley. — 1st Anchor Books
ed.
        p.   cm.
    I. Title.
    [PS3563.A517C63   1999]
    813'.54—dc21   98-48920
                                                              CIP

ISBN 0-385-49420-3

10   9   8   7   6   5   4   3   2   1

for
Kathryn Lucille Needham
1910-1977

The Spirit of Man is descended not only from the Stars and the Elements, but there is hid therein a Spark of the Light and the Power of God.

—Jacob Boehme

THE COCKFIGHTER

~ ONE ~

THE BOY WAITED until the moon rose and the aluminum frame of the window beside him was full of cold light. He watched as it crept up on the bed, across the quilt his mother made—a crazy quilt with no discernible pattern except for a streak of electrified red that appeared as if by accident and must have been the real inspiration behind it. When the square of light got to where his body was outlined underneath the quilt and he could see the slash of red that ran up the middle, defining him, he got up and crept down the hall.

The linoleum was cold and slick. It felt like the hard skin on his heels. The oil heater was turned down low, but the living room was still warm. He went to the door and eased it open, inch by inch, as he had been doing every night for the last couple of weeks. When he was certain that no one had heard, he stepped out on the concrete steps. The cold hit him in the chest like a hammer. It almost took his breath away. Then he forced himself to ignore it. He went down the steps across the gravel where the truck was parked, then on to the gash the bulldozer cut when they leveled off the side of the hill to move in the trailer. There wasn't a flat piece of land to build on anywhere around. It was all up and down. The cut was ten or fifteen feet high and just as raw as when it was made eight years ago. It was pure red clay. Nothing would grow on it. When his daddy put the cages there, it looked as though it was made for them, they fit it so perfect.

His daddy marveled the first time he stepped back and saw it.

And his momma said, That back as far as you can get? She meant from the trailer.

And his daddy said, Yeah, unless she wanted him to go up the hill and down the other side, in which case he might get a little farther away from the house, meaning the trailer, except for the fact that he didn't own over there, and they might not want him coming in on them.

And she said, That'd be all right with me. The farther the better. She didn't want to smell any chickens.

And his daddy said, Why not? It's like perfume, Lily—like Evening in Paris French perfume.

There were twenty of them all together, lined up in one long row in front of the raw clay of the bank. The cages were made out of chicken wire and scrap lumber and set up on legs three feet high so foxes and rats and dogs couldn't get at them. They might have been genuine game cocks, but as far as animals like that were concerned, they were just regular chickens. Underneath the cages the ground was white with their droppings. It looked as though it might have been limed, it was so bright, or, as the boy sometimes thought, an opening had appeared in the earth and the light inside was leaking out. Each of the cages had a couple of milk jugs wired to the side. One was for water, one was for feed. It reminded the boy of a shed full of skulls he saw in a movie.

The Gray was in the first cage he came to. All the others were Clarets, Arkansas Travelers, Butchers, and mixtures of all three or more, bred for speed and guts and endurance, not for the purity of their bloodlines.

There are no thoroughbreds among cocks, his daddy said. They all got the dunghill bred in them along with the gameness, and it takes a hell of a lot of breeding to see they don't revert to the barnyard.

The Gray was the only Gray they had, and when his daddy gave it to him two weeks ago and told him to put it on the keep in preparation for the next derby when he could handle it himself, he couldn't believe it. It was the boy's first cock and the best one his daddy owned, a real champion, the only one that ever won three derbies. It was known for miles around as the toughest, meanest son of a bitch of a chicken there was.

Let me put the gaffs on it, his daddy said, and I'll match any dog in the county. Just put them in a fair fight, that's all.

And the other ones said, What about the dog? You going to allow gaffs on it too?

And his daddy said, Hell no. Why should he? A dog's ten or twelve feet bigger, compared to a cock, and he got natural gaffs in his teeth. He doesn't need them on his toenails too.

And so on like that.

It got so bad the boy was afraid somebody would call his daddy on it and get a dog and blindfold it so it wouldn't know what it was fighting and pit them together, and the dog might make a mistake and eat the cock before the boy got to handle him like his daddy promised.

The boy crept up to the cage so as not to disturb the cock, just as he had been doing ever since it had been put in his care. The bird was sitting on the perch sleeping, its head buried under its wing. The feathers looked like scales of metal shining in the dim, obscure light. They came down in layers from his ruff, where they were darker, more mysterious looking, to the surprisingly light area about the tail. The difference in shading and color made it seem as though the cock was split in

two when it was fighting, flying in two different direc-
tions at once. The boy loved the ruff best. It made the
Gray look like a lion, and that's what he called it. He
did not tell his father about it because his father never
gave a name to a chicken in his entire life.

They're not pets, he told the boy. You want pets, get
your momma to buy one at Easter and raise it by hand.
These are wild animals.

What you call a deer, he said, you see it running in
the woods, lifting its scut?

It was the first lesson his daddy ever taught him, and
he looked at him, not knowing what to say.

Say *Deer*, his momma said.

And he said *Deer*, just like a child, repeating it after her.

And his daddy said, The little shit. Listen to that
little son of a bitch, Lily. And he ruffled the boy's hair
the same way the boy had seen him ruffle the head of
a rooster.

Say it again, you little shit.

The boy said *Deer*, just like he taught him.

And his daddy said, Damn right! And these are cocks.
Remember that. Deer and bear don't have names, and
these don't either, except what God gave them, and
that's enough. You call them *cocks*.

The boy said, Yes, sir.

But his momma said, God didn't name them. Adam
did. And she got out the Bible and read what it said:

And out of the ground the Lord God formed every beast of the field, and every fowl of the air; and brought them unto Adam to see what he would call them: and whatsoever Adam called every living creature, that was the name thereof. And Adam gave names to all cattle, and to every fowl of the air, and to every beast of the field.

That don't include chickens, his daddy said. Chickens don't fly.

But his momma was right. That was the second lesson he learned. The first one was easy, but it took a long time to learn the second because there wasn't anybody to teach him. He had to learn it by himself.

The Gray was his, though. His daddy gave it to him and told him to put it on the keep and get it ready for the next derby, and he could handle it himself. It was his bird. But he was still enough of a boy not to be able to conceive of it even without thinking of it in terms of a name. It was too important to him. He loved it too much. It would be like having a child of his own and not ever naming it, just calling it *Child*.

The Gray's name was Lion. The ruff told him that the same way the rest of them were called cocks because that's what God named them. What else could they be? It was inconceivable to think of them as anything else. The name was part of their real nature, and so was Lion's. His daddy didn't have to know. It was a secret.

He squatted down beside the cage and rested his forehead on the wire. He felt it tremble when Lion shifted. He looked up, and the bird had its head turned to face him. The head rotated, and its ancient eye looked out. The eye was so dark that there was no light reflected in it. It looked like a hole or vacancy—an opening to the void. Then it blinked. The wrinkled eyelid shut and opened, then shut again. The bird slept, and the boy stayed there with it, not caring how cold the night had gotten. He could not have said what he was doing. Perhaps he was keeping guard over it. Perhaps he was simply being there with it, enjoying its presence just as some men enjoy the presence of a beautiful woman and others seek out the presence of God, asking nothing more than to be with Him.

The boy and the cock were both still and unmoving. The cold crept over them both. They were both white in the moonlight, and the boy felt something drain away from him. All the warmth he had brought out of the house with him was slowly leaving his body and dissipating in the cold night air. But at the same time something else was flowing into him, filling him up. Something was spinning off the white sheen of the feathers and the cold translucent light of the moon and entering him, and he could not have said what that was either. The closest he could have come was that it was almost like praying, or worshiping

something. The boy was white and ghastly looking in
the moonlight. The bird was housed inside the tem-
ple, in the tabernacle itself. Half of it was in the light,
the other half was in darkness. It was like a mystery.
The boy knelt in front of it holding the wire with
both hands.

Then he got up and ran as silently as he could back
to the house. Soon it would be dawn, and the seed of
light that the boy believed the cock had within it
would flare in the sun, and it would start crowing.

Later the boy would take the same seed and set it on
fire in the pit.

THE BOY WOKE a few hours later to the sound of
voices buzzing in the wall beside his bed. He looked at
the window. The sky was dark. The moon had set, and
it was near day. He thought at first it was the TV. Then
he heard his mother speak.

"I didn't know you gave it to him."

His daddy grunted the way he did.

"What did you do that for?"

"Because it's time."

"Time for what?"

"Time for you to let go of him, that's what."

"I'm not holding him."

"He won't get hurt."

"How do you know?"

His daddy didn't say anything for a while. Neither did his momma. He could hear himself holding his breath. He felt the thudding in his chest getting louder and louder.

Then his momma said, "Leave him be."

His daddy didn't say anything.

"You hear what I said?"

"I heard what you said."

The boy started to get up and put his ear to the wall to hear better, but he was afraid they might come in and catch him. It was getting him real tense. He didn't want to stay home with his momma.

"It's too rough," his momma said. "Men and women like that."

"Like what?"

"Drinking and whoring and fighting and gambling. I don't want my child there."

"He isn't a child. You seen his pecker?"

"Don't talk like that! Don't ever dare talk to me like that."

"How come? I thought you might be interested in that."

She didn't answer.

"I said, I thought you might be interested in the fact that boy got a pecker almost as big as mine is now. But you ain't interested in that, are you, Lily? Peckers never been high on your agenda."

"Not my son's."

"Husband's neither. You ain't much on peckers, Lily. Never have been. That's the main complaint I got about you."

"You don't have anything to complain about me. I've been a good wife to you, Jake. You get what you want to."

"What about you? That's what I mean. You ever get what you want, Lily?"

"We aren't talking about me," she said. "We're talking about Sonny."

"Don't call him Sonny. He don't like you to call him Sonny."

"You teach him that?"

"What? Hell, no! Listen—I don't have to teach him a thing. He's thirteen Goddamn years old."

"Twelve and a half."

"Who gives a shit? You know what I mean. It's happening, Lily. I don't have to do a thing. I just tell him where to point it, see it don't go off half-cocked."

He started laughing.

The boy laughed too. He had to put his head under the covers, he was laughing so much. He loved his daddy. Ever since a few months ago, when his daddy started paying attention to him, he loved him more than he loved anything, except Lion. It was as though his daddy was waiting for him to grow up. High spirits and high old times—that's the kind of person he was.

When he was little, his daddy had to leave him home with his momma.

That's the woman's part, his daddy said. They're supposed to take care of babies. But now you're grown up and getting balls on you, we're going to be buddies.

He thought to himself, That's all he wanted. There wasn't anything he wanted more than that. When he was a child, he thought like a child, and now he wasn't—like in the Bible.

He pulled his head out from under the covers.

His momma was saying, "Don't talk like that!" and going on about how disgusting he was, always talking dirty like that. She was trying to have a serious conversation.

"I don't want him to turn out like you."

His daddy quit laughing. Neither one of them said anything for a while.

Then his daddy said, "Like what? You mean disgusting?"

She said, "I'm sorry. I'm just upset."

"Like what?"

She didn't answer.

"Answer me, Lily. Talking about peckers, fucking, or what? Fucking upset you?"

"I didn't mean that. You know what I mean. He's just a child. That's what I've been trying to tell you. He's just a baby. You're rushing him too much. You're too rough."

"What you mean *rough?*"

"You know what I mean."

"You still carrying on about that? I told you about that. I'd been drinking."

"I didn't mean that. I meant all the rest of it."

"The rest of what?"

"The whole thing. The way you do. You're one kind of person, and I love you for it. I wouldn't want you to be any different. You believe that, don't you, Jake? You do what you do because that's what you are. I knew that when I married you. But he isn't like that. He's different from you. He's more like me. I'm the one raised him."

"I raised him too."

"You know what I mean. You were off carrying on. That's what I mean. You live rough, and it shows, Jake. Anybody looking at you knows that. Look how you look."

"What do you mean?"

"Look what you got on."

"What's the matter with it?"

"It's just rough, that's all. Nothing's the matter with it. It's just rough."

"It ain't dress up. That's what you mean. I ain't dressed up to go to a party."

"You aren't dressed up at all," she said. "You're dressed to go fighting."

"Damn right. You don't get dressed up to go to a cockfight unless you're Benny Easley, maybe."

Benny Easley was the county commissioner and the only man ever known to go to a cockfight dressed up in a suit and tie. He always said he had an appointment later—an important appointment.

An appointment with the undertaker, they said— Haw! Haw!

The men who said that might have been joking, but they still didn't like it. They didn't like Benny coming in there dressed up in a suit and tie. His daddy said it made them feel too rough.

"Benny Easley knows what he's doing," his momma said.

"If he ever got his head out of his ass, he might. I want some more coffee. It's about time to get going."

It was quiet for a minute.

Then she said, "You know what you look like?"

"Yeah," he said. "I know what I look like."

"You look like you're going hunting, that's what. You look like a soldier. What you trying to hide from, Jake?"

"Hide? That ain't hiding. That's camouflage, that's all. You know why I got these coveralls on?"

She didn't answer.

"It's cold in the pits, that's why. They're insulated. These are insulated hunting clothes. That's how come I got them on."

"You give him a gun?"

"What?"

"I said, 'Are you going to give him a gun?'"

"If he asks me, I will. I won't buy it for him. I'll make him earn it for himself, but I'll go with him and pick it out. Then I'll show him how to shoot it. You know I will."

"I know you will."

"Damn right, I will. When the time comes, I will."

The boy could hardly believe his ears. It had never even occurred to him to wish for a gun, but now that his daddy mentioned it and his momma didn't seem to mind, that's all he wanted. It was like setting a fire to dry leaves. He already had a cock. All he needed now was a gun. Growing up was the most exciting thing that ever happened to him. Every day it was something new. Today him and Lion, next month a gun. He was going to work and get it. Benny Easley would give him a job. He owed his daddy. He didn't know what for exactly, but he knew he owed him.

His momma was still carrying on about something. He could hear her through the wall, but he wasn't listening. He didn't care what she said any more. She was like a hundred-pound weight dragging him back. If she'd had her way, he'd be a girl.

That's what his daddy told him one time.

She always wanted one, he said.

The boy asked him, How come?

And his daddy said, Well, she don't like men.

He laughed and said, Except me. She likes me all right. That's how come she married me. But she don't like the general run of them. They're too rough.

And the boy said, What about me?

And his daddy said, You aren't a man. I'm talking about men. I'm not talking about little children. They're all pretty much the same when they're little, girls and boys both, until they grow up. Then they get different. And I don't mean between the legs. I mean up here—and he tapped his head. Their thinking's all screwed up. You're going to have to wait a while. You're still something in between. She might like you all right till you change. Then you're going to start having some problems. Women ain't men, and they don't much like them. They love them all right. That's how come they get married to them. God saw to that. But they don't much like them. It's like in the Bible, putting the beasts in the Ark together. That's a miracle in itself.

The boy loved his momma and knew she loved him, but he was going to have to change. He could feel it already happening, busting out in him. There was no way he could hold it back any more than he could hold back a season or keep the leaves from coming out on the trees. He didn't want to have to lose his momma, but he couldn't help it. He would if he had to. That's why he had a daddy, he figured—to take her place.

His daddy was talking again on the other side of the wall, and the boy quit thinking about all that.

"You know what's the matter with you, Lily? You worry too much, that's what. If you didn't worry, you'd be all right."

"If I didn't worry, I wouldn't be nothing."

"What the hell's that supposed to mean?"

"I don't know."

"I know you don't. Half the stuff you say, you don't. That's another thing about you, Lily—you talk too much. I'm going to go get him."

"Let him sleep. Go get Homer."

"He's going to meet us."

"Homer'll help. You don't need him."

"I don't need him to help. You know what Homer is?"

"I know it."

"A son of a bitch, that's what. A no-good, Goddamn son of a bitch, that's what."

"I know it."

"If he wasn't your brother—"

He broke off.

"I'm going to go get him."

The boy heard him coming down the hall and pretended to be asleep. He came in the room and shook the mattress, lifting one end of it out of the frame and shaking it up and down.

"Get up, you little fucker," he yelled. "It's time to get up and go get them cocks."

He was ruffling the boy's hair and shaking his shoulders. Then he gave him a knuckle rub.

It hurt so much the boy rolled over and pretended to wake up.

"What time is it?"

The window was still dark. Out there in the night Lion was waiting. He did not think of the cock as caged any more than the sun was caged or a spark of the spirit of God could be caged. The sun would begin to stir in the darkness, and the cock would start crowing. That's what it was waiting for. Part of it didn't ever sleep. It was the seed the boy imagined it had in its heart, the kernel of fire like a bright grain of corn, a piece of the everlasting sun, that let the cock know when it was coming. It was the same thing that made it steadfast. Of all the animals in the world, his daddy said, the cock and the lion are the only ones steadfast, and the boy believed that was so because of the piece of Himself that God had put in them when He fashioned the clay and filled it with His own power and glory.

"Time to get up," his daddy said, and left the room.

"You want you some breakfast, you better get going," he yelled down the hall after he left.

The boy jumped up and looked for his clothes. He was still putting them on when he went in to breakfast.

"Take your time," his momma said.

"Time, hell," his daddy said. "We got to get going."

"The boy's got to eat his breakfast."

"He should have thought about that before. Come on out when you finish," he said to the boy. "I'll be getting them in the truck."

"They haven't even waked up yet," the boy said.

"How the hell you know that?" his daddy said. "That boy's a fucker, ain't he, Lily?"

"Don't talk like that."

"Because they aren't crowing yet," the boy said.

"They will be," his daddy said. "By the time you get finished, hell, I'll be gone."

He put on his old field jacket, the one with the screaming eagle he claimed was a fighting cock on the shoulder. First Airborne Screaming Cocks. He jammed a hunting hat on his head. It was orange and insulated and looked fat, like it was made out of biscuit dough that rose up inside the cloth. He bought one for him and one for the boy the day he told him he could help with the cocks. His momma said they looked like Orange Crush, but that was just her, mocking it. The hats were something between him and his daddy. The boy's was too big, but he lined it with newspapers, and it fit real good now.

"See you out there," his daddy said, and went out the door.

It didn't close good, and his momma went over and slammed it after him. The cold air had come in the room, and it felt for a minute as though the heater had stalled.

"Sit down," his momma said. "I'll fix you some eggs."

"I don't have time for eggs."

He put a piece of bread in his mouth and stuffed it down his throat with his thumb. Then he went over to one of the chairs they used as a place to pile their clothes on and dug out his coat.

"Where's my hat?" the boy said.

"I'm working on it."

"Doing what?"

"Altering it."

"I don't want it altered. What you mean, *altering?*"

"Making it little."

"I don't want it little. I want it big."

She went and got the hat out of her room and handed it to him.

"Sit down and eat."

"I can't eat. You heard him."

"He'll wait a while. He ate *his* breakfast."

"No, he won't. Why didn't you wake me?"

"I wanted to let you sleep."

She was looking at him the way she did some-times—as though he had done something he wasn't sup-posed to, and she was real disappointed in him. He hated it. He didn't need breakfast. His daddy would buy him a bar-b-que sandwich to eat when they got there.

Just then he heard the first cock crow. He was sure it was Lion. Then another. Then all the cocks were crow-ing together like some kind of crazy machine going off. It sounded like a Jubilee. He didn't know what a Jubilee was, but that's what it sounded like.

They ever ask you what a Jubilee is, his daddy said, you tell them that.

And the boy believed him. He'd figure out what it was later on, when he caught up with all the rest of the stuff he was learning.

He started to go out the door, and his mother ran over and grabbed his arm.

"Let me get you something to take."

She looked around as though she was scared, search-ing the table for something to give him. There was nothing there but a dirty plate with streaks of yellow egg yolk on it and a couple of crusts of toast his daddy always left when he finished.

His momma used to say that was the only neat thing about him, the way he ate toast, nibbling the edges off.

And he'd say, Neat? You want to see neat? and pretend like he was unzipping his pants.

That's how his daddy was, always joking and having him a high old time. His momma said he was full of high spirits. That's why the boy loved to be with him. It wasn't all chores. That was the difference. As far as he could see, that was the main difference between a man and a woman. Women worried, and men had fun.

His momma looked at him and smiled. She was still holding his arm, and he was trying to pull away.

"What about a choke sandwich?" she said.

"I don't have time."

"You don't have time for a choke sandwich?"

She was laughing when she said it because it was a joke. One time he was eating too fast. He was always eating too fast, according to her, only this time it was a peanut butter and jelly sandwich, and he couldn't seem to get it down.

Do like a dog, his daddy said. Like this, and he thrust his neck out and pretended to swallow, choking it down the way dogs do, not even chewing.

The boy tried, but it still wouldn't go down. It was like chewing a mouthful of tar. The peanut butter stuck to his teeth, and his tongue dried up and got in the way until he finally couldn't tell it from the rest of the stuff he had in his mouth. It was like a whole wad of mush. All he knew to do was keep chewing.

Drink some water, his momma said, and he drank some water and got it down, and ever after that they called it a choke sandwich. It was his daddy's idea. He did the choking, but it was his daddy's idea about what to call it. He said the boy would have died on the spot if it was the desert and there wasn't any water to wash it down.

"I don't have time for that," the boy said. "You heard what he said. He's fixing to leave."

The worried look came back on her face. He figured it was going to suck him up in a minute, just like a vacuum cleaner sucking up dust and dirt in the corner, if he didn't get out of there. He didn't have time to worry about her and him too.

"I'm all right," the boy said to console her. "I got me some bread."

He held up another piece of light bread and showed it to her.

"Let me get you some more," his momma said, rushing to the table.

As soon as she turned her back, he opened the door and ran out. He ran down the steps and kept on running. The cocks were still crowing, and the sun was just about coming up, and he was running across the gravel to get there before his daddy went off and left him.

HE WASN'T more than halfway there when he saw the truck and the light in the outbuilding where they kept the tackle and realized there wasn't much chance of being left behind. His daddy hadn't even started yet. The boy slowed down to a walk and started eating the piece of bread, listening to the row of cocks in their cages crowing together. His daddy said it sounded like music. He said that about coon dogs too, but the boy didn't know what he meant by that. It sounded like barking and baying to him. But walking along in front of the cages with that many cocks crowing at once, he could see it was like some kind of music. It made his bowels stir and his stomach turn over and a wild excitement begin to build up in him. He was thinking about what they were going to do. He was going to handle a cock—his first cock. And it wasn't his daddy's. It was his own. His daddy already gave it to him, and not only that, it was a champion, a three-time winner. That cock was worth three thousand, eight hundred and fifty dollars in prize money it already won, and there was more coming, his daddy said. No wonder he was excited about it.

He got to Lion's cage and stopped. The cock was busy grooming itself, picking mites and flakes of skin, digging deep inside its feathers. The boy started to say something to get its attention. But he was afraid his daddy might hear him. He dragged his finger across the wire, and the cock quit picking itself and looked up. Then it puffed up its chest and started crowing. The ruff on its neck stood out like it did when it was fighting, and its head was flung back furiously, and the cry that was coming out of its throat was different sounding from all the others—higher and shriller and crazier sounding, full of rage and fury and all sorts of other things the boy couldn't even identify yet. He was thrilled by the passion and violence of it. He took it as a personal greeting, the way he would a dog who was jumping up on him in the morning trying to lick him and running around in circles barking, it was so happy to see him. The boy stood there and received what he thought was the cock's homage for feeding it and grooming it and getting it ready to fight. It was like a salute—a gesture across the great abyss that separated them from each other. He could feel his own spirit rising in him, and he felt it go forth in a flash of excitement.

When the cock was finished crowing and went back to picking and grooming itself, the boy discovered that he still had a piece of bread in his hand. He started to give it to the bird, then checked himself, remembering what his daddy said about feeding it scraps. It wasn't a hog, it didn't eat garbage.

The boy crammed the bread in his own mouth and hurried to the shed, where his daddy was getting the equipment ready. He should have known that's what he'd be doing instead of loading up the truck. His daddy loved the equipment and trappings and all the paraphernalia and rituals of getting ready just about as much as he loved the birds—maybe more.

Trappings are what makes it special, he said. If it was just up to the cocks, they'd fight anywhere, in a pit or on a dunghill. It doesn't make any difference to them. They do it by instinct. It's men that put the art in it, he said. That's the only thing that makes it worthwhile. If it was just chickens killing each other, it wouldn't be worth a shit, but knowing the rules and working the chickens, bringing something out of them they didn't even know was there—that's what makes it so interesting.

What about the cocks? the boy said. They're interesting, aren't they?

Of course they are, his daddy said. You use the cocks. That's where all the art comes in. They got all that bravery and steadfastness in them, and that's what you use.

The boy didn't know what he meant. He wanted to ask him, Use for what? but he was afraid to. The main thing to him was owning a cock and getting to fight him. He didn't even think about the money the way his daddy did. It was the praise and glory he wanted. His daddy talked about all that art, and he tried to listen and do like he said, but it didn't seem to make much sense. Dubbing was dubbing. Trimming was trimming. Exercise was all right. He could see the value in that. But putting a cock on a keep and giving it secret things to eat didn't make sense to him. And knowing how to think like a chicken—that didn't make any sense at all. Not when it came to fighting, it didn't. Fighting was natural. Put cocks together, that's what they did. There wasn't any art to it at all. It was just instinct. That's how it seemed to him. But he was willing to admit that his daddy knew about things he had never even thought of yet. That's why he had a daddy, he figured—so he could teach him. The art was still a mystery to the boy, but he believed in it anyway, the same way he believed in God.

The door to the shed was standing open. The yellow light spilled out in the yard and blocked off a square, like another room in the darkness.

The boy stepped up on the concrete block and went in, still chewing.

His daddy looked up. He was honing a gaff on an Arkansas stone.

"She keep you for breakfast?"

The boy shook his head no.

"What the hell you eating then?"

"A piece of bread."

"That all?"

"Yes, sir."

"You hungry?"

"No, sir."

His daddy smiled.

"About to shit your pants, ain't you?"

The boy thought about the way his bowels stirred and his stomach turned over, but he didn't say if that's how he was or not.

"Polish these gaffs. I'll get the rest of it."

The boy didn't see the sense in that either. They already looked polished to him, and they worked the same way, rusty or bright. He took them out of the crushed velvet compartments inside the gaff box and rubbed them one by one with Brasso. Then he polished them with a clean rag and returned them to the box and snapped the lid shut. When it was closed, it looked like a briefcase. His daddy even had his name on the top near the handle. It was stamped in gold on black imitation leather: SNAKE NATION COCK FARM, JAKE CANTRELL, PROP. Snake Nation was the name of the mountain that rose up behind the cages. The boy didn't know why they called it that. He imagined there were dens of snakes, whole nations of snakes, all over it. But his daddy said it was the name of an Indian town. That's why it sounded sort of peculiar—like Turnip Town or Seteuge Town. They were all names of Indian towns.

The boy didn't know what PROP. meant either, but he figured it must have something to do with all that stuff his daddy took with him. If it was up to him, he'd just take the cocks. That's what it was all about anyway. The trappings just messed it up, distracting attention away from the birds to the men trying to make an art out of it, running around, losing their money and getting drunk and cussing each other. That's how it seemed to him, sometimes. The cocks were pure. They didn't need all that stuff to go with it. His daddy had a couple of boxes full of pills and ointments and medications and waxed string to tie on the gaffs and spur saws and scissors of all sorts of different sizes for all sorts of different things. Each one was special. That was the first thing the boy learned. You don't cut the spurs with the hackle scissors. You want to trim the comb a little, dub him out, you use the dubbing scissors his daddy had set aside in a special place just for that purpose.

His momma used to say she wished his daddy was as neat about his person as he was about those cocks.

He said, If I had a reason to do it, I might. Cocks, I got a good reason for it.

And she'd ask him what, and he'd try to tell her, but she couldn't understand what he was talking about any more than the boy could.

It all seemed made up to him. Most of the stuff his daddy went on about didn't matter a hill of beans. He'd been helping him six months now, and he could see it didn't matter. A cock's going to fight like he's going to fight no matter what you do to him or what kind of art you try to work on him.

But as soon as he thought something like that, he always put a check on it before he got too far. He was just beginning to realize that things aren't always what they seem. Take the world, for example. He always thought it was probably flat. That's how it seemed to him. But people who knew about things like that said it was round, and he believed them. He believed whatever they said. And the same thing was true about his daddy. He believed whatever his daddy told him, even if it didn't make any sense.

The boy closed the box and put up the Brasso. It and the rags had a special place too. Everything in that room was special. He did what his daddy told him to do, but he didn't see any sense in it.

He told his daddy that one time, and his daddy said, You will. Just wait. There's a whole lot more to it than giving them feed.

"That got it?" his daddy said, meaning the gaffs.

"Yes, sir."

"Then get the boxes and start loading up. I'll put this stuff in the truck."

By this time the morning was bright with the sun that spilled over Snake Nation Mountain. The truck and the trees and the gravel were gold.

The boy went to the cages and stopped, confused. Except for Lion he didn't know which cocks to get. He stood there feeling ignorant, not knowing what to do.

He started to call for his daddy, but then he saw Lion and went over to stand beside him. He thought maybe the cock would see him and crow again. The cock looked at him and shifted from one foot to the other. Then it jumped down from its perch and started scratching the wire on the floor of the cage as though it was dirt. It took a shit, and the boy wondered where that came from. The cock was on keep to get it ready for fighting, and they hadn't fed it since yesterday morning.

He was still considering the problem when his daddy came up.

"What happened?" he said. "Where the hell are you?"

"I didn't know what to do," the boy said.

"Get away from that cock, like I said. You don't want to get them used to you. Standing there with your thumb up your ass looking at them like it was a girl showing her tits, they turn into chickens. You want to turn him into a chicken?"

"No, sir."

"Then get away from him, like I said. Leave him alone."

The boy didn't answer. He started moving off to the left, away from his daddy.

"You hear me?"

"Yes, sir."

"It takes the edge off. That's what I'm saying. The less they see of human beings, the wilder they are, and the wilder they are, the better they fight. What the hell you think we breed them for?"

The boy didn't know.

He said, "Yes, sir."

"Let's go then," his daddy said.

He picked up two traveling boxes and told the boy to get the others and then went down the line, loading up the cocks he wanted. They got to Lion, and the boy just stood there. He wanted to load it, but he didn't know if his daddy would let him.

"What the hell you standing there for?" his daddy said. "Load him up."

The boy smiled at him, he was so thankful. But his daddy was already walking back to the truck, a loaded traveling box in each hand.

The boy reached in with one hand and slipped it under Lion's belly, fingers spread between the cock's legs. He was practicing handling. That's the way he'd pit him later, except it was backwards. The cock wouldn't be facing him. It would be facing the other cock, trying to get at him. The cock kept lifting up on its toes, backing up and looking down at the hand sliding up under him. It was too close in the cage to fly. The boy backed him up and got a good grip on him. He lifted him out, and instead of putting him in the case, he held him in his arms a minute, pressing him against his chest with both hands the way he would a cat or a puppy. He glanced over to check on his daddy. Then he bent over and burrowed his face inside the cock's feathers. It smelled dry like something inside a barn—hay or mice or harness leather. He held him there a minute, not knowing what he was doing or why he was doing it or what he wanted. Then he put him in the traveling box and closed the lid on it. He could see the cock looking out at him through one of the airholes. He picked it up and got the box with the other cock and ran over to the truck.

"Goddamn it!" his daddy yelled when he saw him coming. "Don't run with those chickens! You'll shake them up!"

The boy stopped running and slowed to a walk.

"I told you about that," his daddy said when he got to the truck. "You don't ever run with a cock, you hear?"

"Yes, sir."

"Well, set them in there."

His daddy went around to the cab and got in and started the truck while the boy put the traveling boxes in the bed behind the cab, just like his daddy told him to, out of the wind. He got a rope and tied the boxes down so they wouldn't go sliding around, then picked up Lion's box and went to the passenger's side and got in.

"What the hell's that?" his daddy said.

He was already backing up to turn around when he saw what the boy had in his lap.

"What the hell you doing with that?"

But the boy didn't get a chance to answer. As soon as his daddy started the truck, his momma had come running out of the trailer. She ran down the steps across the gravel, holding her hand out in front of the truck to keep it from running over her. She ran around to the passenger's side and opened the door. The boy thought she was getting in. Then he thought she was coming to get him and keep him home with her after all.

"What the hell you doing, Lily?" his daddy yelled.

"He hasn't had his breakfast. He can't go without his breakfast. I made him some."

"What is it?"

"Peanut butter and jelly sandwich."

His daddy started laughing, and the boy felt ashamed.

"I told her I didn't want any," the boy said.

"It wouldn't matter to her if you did," his daddy said. "She gets something like that in her head, you can talk till you're blue in the face, and she still wouldn't listen. She ain't got good sense sometimes. Stand back, Lily! We're already late."

But she didn't move. He started easing the truck forward. She ran along beside it, holding the door. When it was clear she wasn't letting go, he stopped and turned to the boy and said, "Goddamn it! I told you to get that chicken out of here!"

"Let him alone!" his momma shouted from outside the window. "Don't be so hard. Why do you want to be so hard like that for?"

"I told you, Goddamn it, keep out of this, Lily!"

"Let him alone. Here," she said to the boy, pulling the door open and thrusting her hand in his face. "Eat this sandwich."

"Listen, Lily, we're going to be late. Leave him alone."

"When are you coming back?" she shouted.

"When it's over."

"What time is that?"

His daddy put the truck in gear, and the boy tried to close the door. His momma wouldn't let him at first. Then she let go, and he closed it on her. She ran along beside the truck for a while, trying to keep up. Then it started gaining speed.

"You all be careful, you hear?"

The boy could hardly hear what she said, it sounded so far off. She was still running along beside the truck. All he had to do was turn his head, and there she was, but he hated to see her. She was too crazy looking. He thought maybe she was sick and about to throw up. That's why she was looking like that all of a sudden. Then she was gone. He didn't even turn around to see where she was for fear he might turn into a pillar of salt like it said in the Bible. He kept his eyes straight ahead, watching the road turn through the trees, seeing the sun stuck in among them, streaking one side of the trunks and dissolving the mist that rose from the creek running along in the valley below. It wasn't just a whole new day, it was like a whole new life. He was full of excitement and something else—some other kind of strange new feeling he didn't even have a name for yet. There was no telling where they were going or what they were going to do when they got there.

"I TOLD YOU about that chicken," his daddy said after they were driving along for a while.

"He'll get cold out there."

"Damn right. That's why he's got feathers."

"He's a champion bird," the boy said, thinking fast. "It wouldn't do to let him get cold."

His daddy glanced over at him and smiled.

"You little shit," he said. "That's good—that's real good. You keep on thinking like that, you might make a cocker yet. Keep him warm—that's good. You're thinking like a cock now, boy."

The boy was pleased. He was following his instincts. It didn't do to treat a champion cock like the others. That was just good sense.

"Damn right," his daddy was saying. "That son of a bitch is worth a lot of money. The other ones are mostly all chickens. That one's a real son of a bitch."

The boy put his eye to one of the airholes in the traveling box and tried to look in.

"Don't do that!" his daddy yelled.

The boy pulled back as though struck by a snake.

"I've seen them peck an eye out like that. They think it's a button or piece of glass—some shiny shit like that—and peck at it. Son of a bitch ain't got no sense."

The boy did not know who he was talking about, him or the cock.

They were a mile or two from the house, picking up speed on the downhills, losing it on the uphills, when all of a sudden the boy rolled down the window and threw out the sandwich his momma had made him.

His daddy looked at him and kept on driving.

A little farther on he said, "What you do that for?"

"I'm going to get me a bar-b-que sandwich."

"A bar-b-que sandwich. Where you going to get a bar-b-que sandwich?"

"When we get there."

His daddy looked at him.

"When you start eating bar-b-que sandwiches for breakfast?"

"When I started handling cocks," the boy said.

"You ain't started handling them yet."

"I ain't got a bar-b-que sandwich for breakfast yet neither."

His father looked at him again and smiled.

"You little shit," he said. "You handle that cock, I'm going to buy you a bar-b-que sandwich. I'm going to get you one for breakfast every Goddamn day you want, and that's a promise."

"I don't want it every day. I just want it this one time."

It was like a Jubilee. Throwing that sandwich away was something. He never did anything like that before in his life. His momma would kill him. But she was back there, and he was going off with his daddy, going someplace he'd never been with a champion, almost-four-thousand-dollar, three-time-winner cock in his lap. It called for something. He didn't know what. A bar-b-que sandwich was all he could think of, given what he had to work with. But it was a start like it said in the Bible about eating the food you never ate.

- TWO -

SHE RAN ALONG beside the truck until it picked up speed, then dropped back and chased it a while the way a dog chases a car until she realized it was no use. She stopped then in the middle of the road and watched it drive straight into the trees on the edge of the clearing, turn as the road turned, and disappear, going downhill toward the highway. She stood there a while and listened to the sound of the engine. As it faded away into the distance, it seemed to become transformed, almost imperceptibly, into the oncoming light, until finally even the woods were filled with its brightness, and the only sound she could hear was the soughing of the cold, bitter wind and an occasional bird rooting in the dead leaves on the edge of the road, singing the same bleak song over and over. She stood there listening so long that the silence, when it came, was like the perfect counterpart to the cold, bright, glittering air that seemed to be so full of promise that early in the day and yet was so empty, so full of absolutely nothing at all.

She was a shy, quiet woman who had lived without talking most of her life. But after the boy was born, she had gotten so used to the child's chatter, teaching him how to speak, reading him stories, and later, as he grew up, hearing him talk in the other room, listening to the deepening timbre, the maturing masculine sound of his voice, that she had forgotten how lonely she used to be. But now that the silence had come back again, it seemed almost like a relief, it was so familiar. It was like suddenly coming back home after having been away on a long journey and finding herself still there. She had never even left. The whole thing had been a dream.

In her eagerness to give the boy something to eat, she had run out of the house in her nightgown and robe without even pausing to put on a coat. Standing there now, feeling the warmth drain out of her, she suddenly realized how cold it was. She turned and started to run back to the house and hadn't gone more than a step or two when the gravel hurt her feet so bad that she glanced down and saw that all she had on was a pair of thick wool socks she wore about the house. She had knitted them herself from scraps of wool left over from sweaters she had made for the boy over the years. Since none of the scraps were very long, the socks were made up of streaky horizontal lines of all sorts of different colors woven together like Joseph's coat. She picked her way across the gravel as quickly as she could, and when she made it to the steps, she ran in the door and slammed it after her and stood by the heater.

By the time the feeling came back to her feet, they hurt her so bad she sat in a chair and pulled off the socks and examined them. They were swollen and red, and a toenail on her right foot was chipped. She made her way down the hall and got a pillow from the bed and went in the bathroom. She pushed back the plastic shower curtain and sat on the pillow on the edge of the tub and washed her feet, first with hot water and then, when that hurt too much, with cold. Then she patted her feet dry with a towel. She examined them carefully again. The soles were painful to the touch, and she imagined them bruised all the way to the bone. She clipped the raw edges off the chipped toenail and went into the bedroom and put on a pair of thick red kneesocks and a pair of bedroom slippers her son had given her for Christmas one year—a pair of dirty white flannel scuffs with big yellow plastic flowers on top. They were too tight over the socks, the soles were too thin, and her feet hurt to walk in them, so she went into her son's bedroom and got out a pair of his old basketball shoes and put them on without lacing them up. Then she got her winter coat out of the closet and put that on and buttoned it up with cold-thickened fingers and went out in the kitchen and started cleaning up breakfast.

SHE TRIED not to think about it. All the while she was putting up the food and washing the dishes, she tried to think about how much her feet hurt and how her hands ached when she put them in the warm water and how long she could stand to keep them in there without having to pull them out again. She thought about how thick and clumsy her fingers were and how firmly she had to hold the dishes to keep them from slipping out of her hands and falling to the floor and breaking. But nothing she did seemed to help. She still thought about it every few minutes. The boy's face appeared, and she thought about him as if she was in a fever dream between sleeping and waking. She couldn't help thinking about him any more than Homer could help thinking about whiskey when he wanted to get drunk. It was like an obsession. She would think of the boy and picture him at various times in his life like a series of photographs in an album—seeing him asleep in bed or smiling at her across the table or looking up from a book he was reading, his hair a glory in the light of the lamp. She kept imagining in great graphic detail where he was then, at that very minute, and how dark and cold it was in there, and how bad it smelled, full of dust and feathers, and where he was going after that and what he was going to do when he got there and how he would feel. And she wished it was her, not him, having to do it.

She kept picturing a woman she saw in a magazine one time. It was a war somewhere in Asia, and the woman was running down the road, screaming. She was holding a child in her arms. You couldn't tell if the child was dead or not. All you knew was that the woman was screaming.

SHE FINISHED the dishes and dried her hands. They were red and swollen, but they didn't hurt as much as they did. They were mostly hot and itchy now. She figured she was going to be all right. She was just anxious and afraid. Nothing important was going to happen. They would come back, and everything would be just like it had been—except she knew in her heart it wouldn't.

It would never be the same again.

She went in the bedroom and hung up her coat and wondered what she was going to do now—not just for that day, but for the rest of her life. She lay down on the bed and covered herself with a quilt she made a couple of years ago. The pattern was called the Flying Geese. It was made up of a series of small triangles set up on edge. She remembered the boy telling her it looked like the wind got under them and lifted them up like roofing shingles.

She closed her eyes and tried to sleep, but she was too tired. Her mind was too bright, her thoughts were too feverish. She opened her eyes and looked around the room. Everything had an edge to it as though someone had taken a pencil and drawn a line around it, outlining it with light. Pretty soon her head would start aching, and she wouldn't be able to get up for hours. She would just have to lie there seeing the flashes of light that looked like pain and felt like pain and probably was the pain she was feeling. Her heart ached more than her head. She didn't think she would be able to get up anyway, or would even want to.

She thought about the first years of her marriage to Jake and how she thought then that marrying him was the best thing that had ever happened to her. He could have had anyone else in the world he wanted, but he chose her, and she was so grateful she wasn't ever going to let him forget it or think he might have made a bad bargain. She was going to do whatever he wanted, and then some. She clung to him as though she had just fallen off the edge of a cliff and was barely hanging on to the ledge. She was afraid to let go for fear it would kill her.

She was not a very attractive girl. Her figure was all right, but her face was too plain, and she never knew how to fix herself up. Her mother had died when she was a child, and she'd never had anyone to teach her all the practical things a girl has to know, such as how to dress and fix her hair and choose her friends and learn how to dance. She made it up as she went along, and sometimes it worked, and sometimes it didn't. If it wasn't for her breasts—which grew so large when she was a girl that they attracted a lot of attention and gave a false impression of her sexual nature—she would have never had a chance with someone as popular as Jake.

He was full of energy, always joking and carrying on, greedy for life in a way that she never was and never would be. He took things as they came along and wrung the most out of them, and when it was over, he moved on and tried something else. She, on the other hand, was much fiercer than that. She wasn't able to love many things, but those that she did, she loved with the same intensity with which her father loved the harsh God he worshiped. She loved them with her whole heart and soul and every fiber of her being.

Whatever lessons she learned from her father, she carried forth into her marriage and discovered them repeated there. She had grown up to be a good woman. That's what everyone said about her. They said it so

often she even came to believe it herself, except sometimes when she first woke up and the terror was in
the room with her, or late at night when she couldn't
sleep and lay as if on the edge of a beach, neither in the
water nor fully on land, but in that strange element
in between, hearing the nearby breakers roar and feeling another life she had almost completely forgotten
asserting itself.

She could feel the pain now and inside the pain as at
its core, at its hidden, secret heart, a coldness and emptiness that was not pain, that was in fact the complete
opposite of pain—a sense of total isolation, loneliness,
and despair that was the worst pain of all because she
felt nothing, only a great sense of desolation, and there
was no cure for that. It would never go away.

HER MIND DRIFTED back to the cockfight. She
thought about all the men sitting on bleachers and all
the others in the pits fighting their cocks and how they
all looked different—every one of them. Some were
short and some were tall, some were young and some
were old, some were ugly and some handsome. But
inside they were all the same. They might have been one
person inside. They thought the same thing, they said
the same thing, they did the same thing. And he would

too when he grew up, the little baby she had held in the arch of her ribs, in the great, sheltering wings of her pelvis. She remembered the verses her father taught her as a child, not knowing if they were a prayer or a promise:

> And he shall cover thee with his feathers, and under his wing shalt thou rest. Thou shalt not fear for the terror by night: nor the arrow that flieth by day: nor the pestilence that moveth in darkness: nor the devil that appeareth at noonday.

She didn't know when she was first married that it would turn out to be like this. She didn't know that if she had a boy and he lived to grow up, her husband would come and take him away from her, and by the time he was fifteen or sixteen, she wouldn't be able to tell them apart. She might as well not even have had him. Might as well plant him in a flowerpot as far as she was concerned.

If it had been a girl, he wouldn't have cared. A daughter would have been hers for the rest of her life. But if it was a boy, and she really loved him, she had to let him become what he was. And that's what hurt her so much now. She loved him so much that she had to let go and lose him. And not just now. She had to do it over and over the rest of her life. She would have to do it forever, giving him up little by little until he wasn't hers anymore.

And then what? What happened then? What happened after Jake took him and turned him into a man like him? Would she still be able to love him then? What she loved about him now was the sweet little innocent child, not what he would turn into later after Jake got through with him. She raised him to be just like her. Folks said he even looked like her. But what about then? What about when he looked like Jake and dressed like Jake and acted like Jake and all the rest of them—all the other men in the cockpits, making up rules as they went along, running around, shouting and yelling and gambling and betting and staking things on it as though they knew what they were doing, being so mean and rough and tough and acting so stupid and thoughtless.

HER MIND floated aimlessly. Thoughts appeared and disappeared and blended with others, and she remembered something she heard at church. The preacher said a woman had twins, and one of them died, but nobody knew it. The woman didn't even know it was twins. One was born, but the one that died stayed up in her and never came out. The preacher said it turned into stone. Every little cell it had in its body turned into stone like a worm in the ocean that died a million years ago and fell to the bottom, and little by little it turned into stone.

Later on, the woman got pregnant and had another baby, and that's how they found out. She passed it along with the other. It looked just like a regular baby. The preacher said it had little ears and little hands and little fingers and toenails and a little bow on top of its lip. Everything was sharp and crisp. There wasn't a dull edge anywhere on it. It was just perfect.

She remembered being too stunned to speak, hearing him say that. She was stunned then, and she was stunned now, remembering. It was like meeting a total stranger and hearing him tell your whole life story up to and including the future.

Pretty soon it would be as though they had walled her up inside. The whole thing would turn into stone. Not just the little baby inside her, like her own dearest twin, but her heart and soul and her tender affections. Little by little it would all turn into stone like that worm in the mud and slime of the ocean. Pretty soon there wouldn't be anything left except her, and inside her, if you broke her open, a perfect little petrified baby—like a jewel. And it would be everything she ever wanted. It would be the perfect child she always dreamed of when she was a girl. It would look just like Jake when he was a boy, not as he was now, when the drinking and running around tore him down, but as he was in the tenth grade, when they first met. And it would be hers. He wouldn't be able to lay a hand on it. He wouldn't even know it was there because he wouldn't be able to see it any more than the woman who had twins was able to see her own little petrified baby. It would be hers. And it would always be with her—flesh of her flesh, bone of her bone. She imagined the great, sheltering wings of her pelvis closing around it, like valves of stone, protecting it from all harm until they became one thing —one man and one woman, one husband and one wife, one mother and one child—one woman, one son.

- THREE -

A HALF HOUR LATER, they were still driving. His daddy hadn't said a word after he promised to buy the boy a bar-b-que sandwich. He was too busy thinking about what he was doing and singing along with the radio, and the boy was too busy thinking about Lion and checking out the scenery. Most of it was houses—what there was of it—and woods and fields with mountains rising up like wild hogs. They passed a house trailer that said *Bar-B-Q,* and another that said *Pete's Eats.* After a while they turned off at New Harmony Baptist Church and went down a dirt road, then another, and then pulled off through an open gate into a pasture. There wasn't a road, just ruts in the grass. They followed the track along the top of a knife-edge ridge with rocky pasture falling away on either side and a house or two in the hollow below. Then it flattened out and began to look more like a field.

A little farther on, they came to where the cars were parked. There were about twenty or thirty of them already there, mostly old American cars and pickup trucks. They were parked anywhere, at all sorts of different angles. It looked as though somebody took them and threw them. Behind the cars were a couple of buildings. One was an old broiler house. It was long and low and had sheets of translucent plastic nailed over the windows. Some of the sheets had torn loose and flapped in the wind and scratched the dry weeds that had grown up along the side. The roof was tin and rusted in streaks like somebody had hacked at it with a knife and it was still bleeding. The sides were covered with black tar paper. It had been torn off in places, and weathered, unpainted boards showed through. The other building behind it was square and looked as though it might have been a store at one time, or a storehouse. The walls were unpainted board and batten oak planks. They looked streaked and weathered too, except in the front. The wall behind the porch looked as though it had been whitewashed at one time.

His daddy drove up as close as he could. At the near edge of where the cars were parked a man in bib over-alls flagged them down.

"That's fifty cents," the man said.

His daddy leaned out the window.

"Since when do you charge for parking?"

"Since just now."

"To hell with it then," his daddy said. "I pay like the others."

"The others paid."

"What about entries?"

"All pay. That's the rules."

His daddy reared back and fished in the pocket of his coveralls. He got out fifty cents and paid him. The man's hand, when he took the coins, looked as big as a dinner plate.

"Where do we go?" his daddy said.

"Go where you want to," the man said, and he waved his hand expansively as though he was offering him the entire world and a permit to park wherever he wanted.

"I mean the cockhouse. I got a load of cocks here."

He held up the briefcase of gaffs. It might have held dueling pistols or corporate papers, the way he acted.

"Snake Nation Cock Farm," his daddy said, reading the gold lettering in case the man might have missed what it said. "Jake Cantrell, Proprietor."

"You the one got that Gray?"

"Damn right."

"Why didn't you tell me? You going to pit it?"

"Damn right."

"I am," the boy said, leaning across his daddy so the man could get a good look at him.

The man looked surprised. He glanced at his daddy, then at the boy, then back again as though he didn't know what to believe and kept on shifting from one to the other trying to figure it out.

"This is my boy," his daddy said. "He's the one going to handle it."

"It's my cock," the boy said, still leaning over his daddy, looking up at the man.

The man started smiling. The boy could see he didn't believe him. He was smiling too much, and the smile looked too false, just like his teeth. He figured he might have to wipe it off for him. Or Lion would.

"Sure it is," the man said.

"Spread it around," his daddy said. "I'm giving odds."

The smile slid off the man's face like oil and settled down around his neck. He looked like he had turkey wattles or big flews on his jaws like a dog.

"You betting on him?"

"Damn right," his daddy said. "Who else would I bet on? I got me a winner."

The boy didn't know who he was talking about —him or the bird. He looked at his daddy and hoped it was him.

"You mean that bird?" the man said, seeking the same sort of clarification.

"Damn right," his daddy said. "That bird's a winner."

"Well, I'm going to watch him," the man said.

His daddy said, "Shit, you better. You'll never see anything like it—a champion cock and a twelve-year-old boy handling him."

"Thirteen," the boy said, but they didn't act like they heard him.

"How much the odds?" the man asked.

"I don't know. Twenty-five, twenty. Talk to me later. I might fight him last. He's a shake."

The man nodded his head real slow. He acted as though there was something in it he didn't want to break by doing it too fast—something real precious.

"I want to see that," the man said.

"Of course you do," his daddy said. "That's why I'm doing it. Spread the word. I got a whole bank I'm putting up on him. Tell them that when they come in."

That's how his daddy did. He made it exciting. That's why the boy loved to be with him.

"That bird's worth four thousand dollars," the boy said, leaning over his daddy again.

The man looked blank, struck dumb by the news.

The boy said it again. The first time had such an effect he figured he ought to repeat it and let the man know the enormity of it.

"That's how much I made on him," his daddy said. "And I'm fixing to make a little more now that I got me a bankroll to do it with—if I can ever get over there and get started. Where's it at?"

"Over there," the man said.

He pointed to the second building, the one behind the old broiler house.

His daddy waved and put the truck in gear, and they drove over to it through ruts in the grass and splotches of cow shit.

When they got to the porch, his daddy stopped the truck and said to the boy, "Get it unloaded. I'm going to go sign us in. You see Homer, get him to help you. And tell that son of a bitch to stay here, don't do a thing till I get back."

"What if he already did?" the boy said.

His daddy smiled.

"He probably did. Just tell him to stay. I'll be right back."

They got out of the truck. The boy set Lion on the front seat. Then he went around and untied the other cases and carried two of them into the house. Inside was one big room divided into plywood cubicles, each with its own bank of cages, a couple of mule ear chairs, and a worktable made out of scrap lumber. The two cubicles nearest to the door were full. The men looked up as he passed. When he saw that the third one was empty, he went in and put the two cocks he had with him in the cages provided. Then he returned for the others. He carried in the rest of the equipment and arranged it on the table the way his father had taught him, lined up in just the right order. Then he went out and got Lion. He took the cock out of the traveling box with one hand, practicing the handle. Then he started stroking his back to soothe him. The cock closed his eyes like a cat, and the boy burrowed his face in the cock's feathers, smelling the intimacy. They stood there a moment. Then the boy put him in the special cage he had chosen, as far from the others as possible. Then he sat in a chair and waited. Down the hall he could hear the men talking. Every now and then a cock crowed or flapped against the sides of his cage. He could hear their toes and the hard skin of their feet on the wires, and he began rehearsing the moves and everything else his daddy had taught him.

He was there about three or four minutes when Homer came in.

"There you are," Homer said. "I've been looking for you."

The boy felt no need to answer. His daddy wouldn't have, so why should he?

"You got it all ready?" Homer said, talking about nothing, as usual. His daddy said he never knew a man to talk as much like a woman as Homer did.

The boy said, "Yeah."

He didn't even look up to see him.

"Where's your daddy?"

"Signing in."

Homer sat down in the other chair. The boy was too far away to smell Homer's breath, so he didn't know if he'd been drinking or not. His daddy wouldn't like it if he'd been drinking. Nobody would.

"You been drinking?" the boy asked.

Homer looked surprised.

"Of course not, you little shit. Who told you to say that?"

"Nobody. I said it myself."

"You little shit, I told your daddy I wouldn't. He said to come help him, cover the bets. I told him I would. He got my word on it. I said, I don't give a shit for cocks. I'll have mine for Sunday dinner. The only way I like chicken, I told him, is cut it in pieces and fry it for dinner. But I don't mind money. I don't mind making money. You got a proposition about money, that's serious business. I don't drink when it's serious business."

It was all lies. The boy knew that.

"I thought you quit drinking."

"I did," Homer said. "Ever since I got out of Detox. He knows that. Your momma knows that. I told him I quit."

"That's good," the boy said.

He did not believe it any more than Homer believed it himself.

They waited a while.

"How long was that?" the boy said.

"What?"

"You get out of Detox."

"Two weeks. A little over."

They waited some more.

"When's he coming?" Homer said.

"When he gets through."

"I want to get started."

"Doing what?"

"Whatever he says to."

"You can't get started till they get started."

He explained it to him as he would to a child.

"I can get started setting it up. I just need the money."

"He'll be along."

They waited some more.

"I hear you're going to handle one of them," Homer said.

"Yes, sir."

"First time."

The boy looked up at him.

"Damn right."

"Your daddy says that's going to set it up. That's going to make us a lot of money. A twelve-year-old boy handling a champion—"

"Thirteen," the boy said, interrupting him.

"You thirteen?"

"Just about."

"Just about's not it. I'm going to say twelve. That sounds better. That's going to attract a lot of attention. Folks going to want to bet on that."

"How come?"

"How come? It's unusual—that's how come. Folks are going to want to bet on the unusualness of it."

"How come?"

"See if you can do it, I reckon."

The boy looked serious.

"I wouldn't do it if my daddy didn't say I could. I wouldn't want to. He said I was ready."

"Of course you are. That's what fools them. That and the fact he's a champion cock. Your daddy said Lily could handle that one, if she could ever bear to touch him, and he'd still win. It ain't the handler, it's the cock."

"They say it's the handler," the boy said. "They say a cock's no good without a good handler."

"That right? Well, I don't know a damn thing about it. I know how to bet. That's all I know. I know how to take folks' money and give them change. Except in this case there isn't going to be any change. Your daddy says it's a sure thing."

"That's right," the boy said, thinking of Lion. In each of the last three derbies he killed his cock in less than two minutes.

"You're damn right, that's right."

"Bet some of your own, your daddy said—if you got some left. That's all right with me. There's going to be enough to go around even with both of us betting on it."

"You got to know a lot about it," the boy said.

"Not for betting."

"I'm not talking about betting. I mean handling. There's a lot to it."

"Is that right?" Homer said.

He leaned over and spit on the floor. Then he sat and inspected it. He didn't seem interested in art like his daddy. He didn't seem interested in much of anything, his momma said, except drinking. He was the black sheep of the family. Every family has a black sheep, and Homer was the one in hers. It made her cry to think about it, and when the boy asked her why, she said, The waste. He's a good man at heart, and look what happened. He wasted his life.

The way she always talked about Homer, it sounded like he was already dead.

He was my pet before he got drinking, his momma said, and even now I can't help but love him.

I can, his daddy said. I don't like the son of a bitch.

He isn't your brother, his momma said. That's why. If he was your brother, you'd love him too.

I doubt it, his daddy said. It takes a man with an awful strong stomach to put up with Homer, let alone love him.

I'm not talking about a man, his momma said. I'm talking about a woman. If you were a woman, you'd love him like I do even if you felt sorry for him.

His daddy said, Shit. And his momma started crying again like she always did when they talked about Homer.

They sat there a while with Homer inspecting the gob of spit as though it was the most fascinating thing he ever saw. It might have been an egg he just laid, the way he was looking at it.

"Daddy says it's an art," the boy said.

"I reckon it is."

He didn't care. The boy could see that. That's how Homer did. He'd be going along, and all of a sudden he'd act like somebody cut him off or put him in neutral.

Homer didn't seem interested in talking to him, but the boy wanted to talk anyway. He was nervous. He couldn't stand to think about it.

"I put him on the keep," the boy said.

"Is that right?"

"You know what that is?"

"What?"

Homer looked up. He didn't seem to know what the boy was talking about.

"I said, I put him on the keep. You know what that is?"

"Not exactly. When's he coming? I got something I got to do."

"Pretty soon. I exercised him. That's one thing. Besides the vitamins and feed. I'd hold him up and make him fly. Strengthen his wings. That makes him strong. That and strychnine."

"What?"

"Strychnine."

"What strychnine?"

"I fed it to him."

"Bullshit! Strychnine's poison. That'd kill him."

Just then his daddy came in.

"It's poison for people," his daddy said, "but not for cocks. You know what's poison for cocks?"

He bugged his eyes as though he had a big surprise coming.

"Sweet milk. That'll kill a cock every time."

"Bullshit!" Homer said.

He looked insulted.

"No, sir," his daddy said. "That's the truth. Sweet milk'll kill them, but strychnine sets them up. It's the opposite from the way it is with people."

Homer acted as though he still didn't believe him.

"Amphetamines," his daddy said. "You ever take amphetamines?"

"I might have," Homer said evasively.

"Same thing. That's how strychnine does to a chicken."

"And vitamin B-12," the boy said.

"That's right," his daddy said. "And Jake's Special Conditioner. You know what that is?"

Homer looked at the boy as if he might be able to tell him. Then he looked down at the spit.

"It grows balls on them," the boy said.

"That's right," his daddy said. "That's how I got a four-thousand-dollar bird sitting right there in that cage waiting to go out and make me more money. I got a special conditioner. My own secret formula."

"He taught it to me," the boy said.

Homer looked up.

"When are we going?"

"As soon as it starts," his daddy said. "Now listen, Goddamn it. This is important. Here's the plan. I handle the first three cocks."

"How many you got?" Homer asked.

"Look there," his daddy said, pointing at the cages. "How many you see?"

"Four," Homer said.

"That's what I got. I put up a hundred dollars to enter. Winner takes all. There're sixteen handlers in the derby. That's sixteen hundred dollars right there, besides what else we take in on bets."

"What you got to do to win it?" Homer asked.

His daddy said, "Shit, you don't know as much as that boy."

Homer looked up. That seemed to get his attention.

"I didn't say I do," he said. "I just asked a question. I don't give a shit about cocks. I told you that. I don't like the fuckers. I'd just as soon fight a snake as a cock."

"You can't fight snakes," the boy said. "They won't fight."

"Who gives a shit?" Homer said. "That's my point. You're missing the point."

"The one that wins the most matches wins," his daddy said, explaining it to him like he would to a child.

Homer nodded.

"All right," he said. "We bet on them all?"

"Just the ones I tell you to."

"Now listen," his daddy said to the boy. "I'll handle the first three birds. That Gray's a shake. I talked to the judges, and they agreed to run them last. Builds up the excitement. That's what they'll be waiting for."

The boy couldn't stand it, hearing his daddy talk about it.

"What's a shake?" Homer asked.

"More than six pounds. All the others fight by weight within two ounces. Shakes, though, it doesn't matter. They put them together. It doesn't matter what they weigh."

"Heavyweights," Homer said.

His daddy nodded.

"Heavyweight chickens," Homer said.

He started laughing.

That's how he was. That was the whole trouble with Homer.

"Listen," his daddy said to the boy. "You help me out."

"Yes, sir."

"I want you to get them ready for me. If they get in the drags, you take over."

"What's drags?" Homer said.

His daddy ignored him.

"Homer and I'll work the crowds, and when it gets to that big Gray, you take over and handle him. We'll do the betting, and you win that fucker, and we'll clean them out."

"What about the other ones?" Homer said.

"The other what?"

"The other chickens. We bet on them?"

"I'll tell you what to bet. A man who doesn't even know what a shake is doesn't have any business betting— ain't that right, boy?"

"Yes, sir."

"Betting's a serious business, Homer. You don't just do it."

"I know that."

"Then act like you do. If you're going to be betting my money, you better listen and do like I tell you."

Homer didn't even look up. He was inspecting the spit again.

"All right," his daddy said. "You got that?"

"What about the money?" Homer said.

"What money?"

"The money to bet with."

His daddy counted him out some money. He went over to the medicine box and got out a pencil and piece of paper and wrote on it and gave it to Homer.

"What's that?" Homer said.

"An IOU. Sign it."

"What for?"

"So I get my money back, that's what. I want a record of what I give you, and I want it back."

"What if I lose it?"

"You do like I say, you aren't going to lose it. That paper says I get back the money I give you plus whatever you make on the bets."

"You don't need that," Homer said. "You got my word on it. Besides, we're family, Jake. It just ain't friendly making me sign something like that."

"Go ahead," his daddy said.

"What do I get? Put that on it."

His daddy took the piece of paper and wrote on it and pushed it back over to Homer.

"Ten percent," his daddy said.

"Plus expenses."

"What expenses?"

"Getting over here and eating."

"That's right," his daddy said to the boy. "You haven't eaten. Homer, you shit-ass, sign the paper, and I'll give you your fucking expenses."

Homer signed the paper.

His daddy said to the boy, "Come on."

Homer got up. "Where you going?"

"Get this boy a bar-b-que sandwich."

"I might have me one too," Homer said, following them out.

- FOUR -

The concession was at one end of the old chicken house. There was a Dutch door with a shelf in the middle. That was the counter. Behind the counter was what looked like a kitchen, but the only thing in the kitchen that wasn't already packaged up was bar-b-que sandwiches.

"It's a little early for bar-b-que, isn't it?" Homer said.

"Don't eat it then," his daddy said.

"I might have to," Homer said. "I didn't have time to get any breakfast, and I can't think on an empty stomach."

"Full one neither," his daddy said, laughing to show he was joking. "You getting expenses—this is it."

They went over to the wood stove under the bleachers and ate what they bought. Beside them, nailed to the back side of the bleachers, was a sign made out of a sheet of six-by-eight-foot plywood painted white with powder blue lettering. It had been there so long that it was covered with dust and cobwebs and looked like it was growing a fungus. The lettering was done by someone who didn't know what he was doing. Some of it was printed, some was in cursive. Some of the lines slanted up, others sloped down. The boy took his bar-b-que sandwich and went over and read it.

```
              PIT RULES
          Everybody pays
        Absolutely no Drinking
   Anyone Drinking will be Barrd
        Watch your Language
        Keep your Bets Straight
         Weigh in by 10:00
       All Derbies Blind Matchd
      Once Enterd in Derby you
         Can Not Withdraw
        absolutely no flat gaffs
      No Quick or rough Handling
    Anyone Buying, Selling a fight

       Or Switching Bands will
              Be Band
       worthman rules used
```

Besides two bar-b-que sandwiches, Homer got four bags of potato chips, a Mounds candy bar, and two small Alabama pecan pies.

"Looks like Detox agreed with you," his daddy said.

"I'm getting it back," Homer said. "I lost my appetite for a while. Besides, I'm eating some of this later."

They threw the wrappers in the fire. The stove was made out of a fifty-gallon oil drum with a hinged door cut in the front with a torch. The pipe went up a little over their heads, turned at a ninety-degree angle, and went out a window. His daddy opened the door of the stove, and the boy could see the fire burning inside. It looked like its innards. The papers the bar-b-que sandwiches came in were slick with grease and smeared with sauce. The boy thought it looked like chicken blood, and his stomach turned over. It was going to start soon.

Then they went over and checked the pits.

There were three of them—a main pit and two drag pits. The main pit was in the middle, and it was about twice as big as the others. They all had dirt floors and were fenced in with hogwire three or four feet high. At one end of the main pit was a gate made of wood and wire and a chair for the scorekeeper. It looked like a lifeguard's chair at the beach. It had slats nailed to the side so the scorekeeper could climb up. Beneath the chair was a shelf on a rail. On the shelf were three or four milk jugs of water, a couple of pencil stubs, a blue spiral notebook, and a pair of butcher scales. The railings and posts the hogwire was nailed to had been whitewashed or painted at one time, but it had just about all worn off. The top rails were slick and greasy with wear, and the bottom rails were covered with dirt from the pits and bits of fluff and chicken feathers stuck in the rough wood. The bleachers were shaped like a V. They came down on either side of the pits, and the rake was so steep they looked like ledges of rock going straight up a cliff all the way from the floor to the ceiling. The seats and the framing were made of rough lumber—unpainted, unplaned oak planks a full two inches thick, cut at a jackleg sawmill nearby. The bleachers were already filling up. The men wore jeans and field jackets and camouflage hunting clothes. They looked like a unit in a rebel army somewhere in Central America. The women were mostly wrapped up in quilts—Bridal Wreaths, Dutch Girls, Baskets of Flowers, Cathedral Windows, Log Cabins, Crazy Quilts. They had them pulled up over their heads like Indian blankets, or tucked in neatly around their legs. Sometimes there were three or four women sitting together laughing and talking. They were gaudy as flowers. The women stood out in the darkness inside like spots of bright sun in the forest.

"Looks good," his daddy said.

"Yes, sir," the boy said, echoing him. "Looks real good."

"Hey, Jake!" one of the women yelled, throwing back the edge of a quilt and waving her hand.

His daddy looked up.

"Come here a minute."

His daddy looked at the boy and said, "Wait here."

But the boy didn't want him to go off and leave him. Not now, not when they just barely got there.

"No, sir," the boy said.

His daddy grinned.

"Wait here a minute," he said to Homer.

He turned, and the boy followed him up onto the bleachers. They climbed them like steps until they got to where the women were sitting.

There were two of them, the one who waved and another just like her. They both were sitting side by side sharing a king-size quilt that was wrapped around their legs in front, tucked in under their haunches, and pulled up over their heads in back. It looked like some kind of Double Ring pattern. The boy didn't know what it was called. Ball Bearings, most probably. Or Chain Link Fence. It wasn't one his momma made.

It's like their imaginations get heated, he remembered his daddy saying. That's how come you don't know what it is.

The women were about thirty-five or forty years old. They had regular features, but they were starting to turn into hard-looking old country women with square jaws and pinched little leathery faces. They had dyed blonde hair with the roots showing through and thin lips with a lot of red lipstick setting them off. His momma would have said they were common, and they probably were, the way they were carrying on with his daddy, cutting their eyes and making up to him. He didn't know why his daddy was wasting their time visiting with them when there were so many other things they ought to be doing.

One was called Roma, the other was called Janelle. The one called Janelle had marital troubles.

"She's been telling me all about them," Roma said to his daddy. That's how come I called you up here, so you could give her a little advice."

"What kind of troubles?" his daddy said, leaning over and grinning in Janelle's face.

"Anything I can help you with?"

The women squealed.

"His name is Daryl," Roma said. "He's a real son of a bitch."

Janelle agreed with her.

"Trouble is," Roma said, "she says she's in love with him."

"I love him to pieces," Janelle said. "I don't care what he does."

"That's the trouble right there," his daddy said, straightening up. "That's how come you got marital troubles. It don't pay to love a man like that."

Janelle didn't even bother to answer.

"The trouble with Janelle," Roma said, "is she married a son of a bitch like Daryl, and all he does is take advantage."

"I don't see why we got to talk about me to a perfect stranger," Janelle said.

"He ain't a perfect stranger, Janelle."

She turned to the boy.

"Why don't you come and sit with us, honey? You ain't interested in that shit, are you?"

She pointed down at the cockpit. Homer saw her and started waving his arm. In a minute he'd come stomping up the seats of the bleachers and crowding in like he always did if they let him.

"I'm sorry, Roma," his daddy said. "We're fighting some cock."

"I don't mean you," Roma said. "I mean him," indicating the boy.

"I can't do it neither," the boy said. "I'm fighting a cock myself. A four-thousand-dollar, three-time champion."

Roma bugged her eyes like she couldn't believe it.

"You know what it is they're doing down there?"

She meant in the cockpit.

The boy nodded his head. Of course he knew what they were doing. He wouldn't be fixing to go down there if he didn't know what he was doing. His daddy wouldn't let him.

"Hey, Janelle," Roma said. "You hear that? He knows what they're doing."

"No, he don't," Janelle said. "Nobody does. That's the problem."

"That's right," Roma said. "There're no rules. It's like Monday Night Football. That's how come you can't understand it. They make it up as they go along. It's all about cocks. You ever wonder why they call them that?"

Janelle squealed. A minute ago her head was swarming with marital troubles, but as soon as Roma mentioned cocks, it seemed like she forgot all about them. That's how it was. She said anyone who could make her laugh had a key to her heart. And Roma said, That ain't all they got a key to. But Janelle didn't care. She said it wasn't her fault if she had a good disposition.

"Go on, Roma," Janelle said. "You're making me embarrassed."

"It's the truth," Roma said. "You ever see how they squat on their haunches and hold those cocks between their legs when they talk?"

The boy was surprised. He had seen his daddy do that.

"You ever see how they sit and play with them?"

"Quit talking like that," Janelle said. "I mean it. You're making me nervous."

"*I* mean it," Roma said. "There's a real connection between them."

Janelle squealed again.

A few rows down some men turned around and looked at her. One of them grinned and waved his hand.

"Don't mind her," Roma said.

Janelle was hiding her face in her hands and peeking out from between her fingers and laughing.

"We're taking about cocks," Roma said.

"Why talk about them?" the man said.

Janelle squealed and hid her face again

"Well, ladies," his daddy said. "We got to be going, much as you'll miss us. We got to go weigh our cocks."

The women squealed and the boy was disgusted. He felt just like Jesus. The Bible said He never laughed. He wept a lot, but He never laughed a day in His life, his momma said, because what He was doing was too serious. There was too much riding on it to be laughing.

His daddy turned and left, and the boy followed him down the bleachers, zigzagging past scattered groups of people. When they got to the bottom, they stepped off onto the pulverized dirt and went over to Homer, who was still standing there where they left him, studying the pit.

"What's the lines for?" Homer asked.

It was like they hadn't even been gone.

"What lines?"

"Down there."

He pointed at the main pit. There were two sets of parallel white lines made with lime like lines on a tennis court.

"Tell him what the lines are for," his daddy said to the boy.

"That's where you pit them," the boy said.

"That's where all the action is," his daddy said. "You keep your eye on that, you hear? Come on, they're starting."

A fat man climbed up in the scorekeeper's chair and called out, "Numbers two and eight, weigh in."

"Come on," his daddy said. "That's us."

"I'll wait here," Homer said.

"Not with all that money you won't. I want you with me—me or the boy, either one. I don't want you going off by yourself."

"I'm not going off."

"I know you're not. Not as long as you're with me you're not. Come on."

His daddy went up to the scorekeeper and got a slip of paper telling which rooster to fight first.

"We're eight," his daddy said. "Remember that."

"Yes, sir," the boy said, eagerly. He was so excited he didn't know what to do. Something inside him was trying to get out. He didn't know what, but that's what it felt like.

They went back to the cockhouse, and his daddy got out the Arkansas Traveler and set him up on the table. Homer held the bird in both hands like a woman would if she had to do it, and the boy attached the gaffs to the spurs on the back of his legs while his daddy trimmed him out. He trimmed the tail a couple of inches, shortened the wing primaries, cut a little off the saddle in back, and trimmed around the vent.

"That ought to lighten him up," he said, stepping back to view his work. "Cool him off so he won't overheat."

He attached the lead band the scorekeeper gave him to the chicken's right leg, picked him up, and put him under his arm like a melon.

"Let's go," he said. "Homer, you bet on this one, you hear? Go up to seven or eight. No odds, you hear me? Even bet."

When they got back to the pit, Homer climbed up in the bleachers and went to work the way the boy knew he would, making a fool out of himself shouting out numbers and taking bets, saying, "Goddamn son of a bitch! Look at that one," pointing down at the boy and his daddy. "I just got to bet on that one. I don't care if I lose or not. Who's going to take it?"

An old man in a Bush Hog cap and no teeth but a real sharp nose nodded his head. He looked like a chicken pecking at something.

Homer said, "You're on. Who's another?"

"You're on," another man said.

Homer climbed over and shook his hand and patted him on the back, moving on, working the crowd like a dog working his way through the bushes, shaking the tops.

"Go up there and tell him to shut up," his daddy said to the boy. "Tell him I said it ain't a show. He's making a damn fool out of himself carrying on like that. Tell him I said to wait till later, after we got it built up a little. He's liable to spend himself too soon and get them suspicious. He ain't having to sell them something they don't already want."

The boy climbed up and delivered the message, and Homer sat down where he was and called his bets from his seat like the rest of them.

"Looked like he was selling peanuts," his daddy said when the boy got back. "What the hell's the matter with him?"

"He doesn't know what he's doing," the boy said proudly, knowing that he did. If he knew that much already and he wasn't but almost thirteen years old, he wondered what he was going to be like when he got to be as old as Homer was. He couldn't even imagine it.

"Damn right," his daddy said. "Son of a bitch takes after your momma. That whole damn family's born with something wrong with them, boy. I don't know what the hell it is. Something's missing. They ain't got a lick of sense. All that preaching their daddy went on with went to their heads."

The boy looked worried. She was his momma. He could have inherited it from her the same way children inherit their mouths or noses. He didn't want to look like her. He wanted to look like his daddy and act like him too, not like her and Homer, going through life with something missing and never even knowing what it was. He imagined it as a body part—a hand or a foot—except it was inside where no one could see it. Some essential organ was missing, something they should have been born with left out. It was his greatest fear that he would grow up and turn into Homer instead of his daddy. He already looked like him because of his momma. What if he started acting like him too?

THE FIRST FIGHT was a clean kill. They set the cocks loose at the far score lines, and they hit one another and flew in the air and bounced off the hogwire. By the time they came down the other cock was already uncoupled. Its spinal column was severed, and it couldn't even use its legs to stand up or crawl. It tried to steady itself with its wings, but his daddy's cock was all over it, jumping up on it and gaffing it until it couldn't move. His daddy's cock got hung up in it, and then neither one of them could move. They lay there on top of each other until the referee cried out,

"Handle," and the handlers moved in and pulled them apart. And that was it. The other cock was already dead.

When they checked with Homer afterward, he had made four hundred and twenty-two dollars, not counting some he claimed was his bet, made on the side with his own money.

They went back to the cockhouse, doctored the cock, which had a puncture wound in his chest that missed its heart by a good half inch. And that was it. They turned back the feathers and checked the cock all over, but they couldn't find another mark on him.

"Keep on like that," his daddy said. "I'm going to have me another champion here."

"Looks like luck to me," Homer said.

His daddy said, "Shit. There's no luck to it, except what you make yourself, Homer. The reason that damn cock's so good is I knew how to breed him. I knew how to put him on the keep."

"That your secret?" Homer said.

"That's one of them."

"Secret feed?"

"It might be."

"You could sell that for a lot of money, a secret formula like that."

"If I was fool enough, I might. But that's not all. It's the handle."

"What handle?" Homer said.

Homer turned to the boy.

"What handle's that?"

The boy just looked at him.

"The handle on a shovel maybe, shoveling bullshit," Homer said. "There's no Goddamn handle. Not in that. Not in what I saw. You turned him loose. You call that a handle?"

"Look at my shoes," his daddy said.

Homer said, "What?"

"What color are they?"

"White."

"Damn right. White shoes. I bought them special. What color the other handler have on?"

"I can't remember."

"That's right," his daddy said.

He turned to the boy.

"You remember?"

"No, sir."

"That's right. You don't remember because they were just shoes, that's all. They blended in. That's what I mean."

Homer looked blank. Something was happening, but he didn't seem to know what it was. The boy didn't either. He felt abandoned. He was on the outside with Homer, looking in.

"What's shoes got to do with it?" Homer asked.

"Everything," his daddy said. "That's the handle."

"What handle?"

"I flashed my shoes at him. He turned that bird loose, and I shuffled my feet like this."

He made a slight movement. His shoes caught in the light and flashed.

"My cock couldn't see it. Because why?"

"Why?" Homer asked.

"He had his back turned," the boy said. He almost laughed, it was so simple.

"That's right," his daddy said. "And that other bird didn't know what it was. He thought it was two or three of them coming—one cock and two shoes. That threw him off just for a second, enough to get a gaff in him."

"That fair?" Homer asked.

"Fair? Shit. He won, didn't he?"

"What about rules?"

"They didn't see me. They got rules about hand-kerchiefs and clucking and blowing and waving your hands, but they ain't got around to shoes. They ain't even thought of that yet. That's what I mean. You don't just turn them loose, see what happens. There's an art to it."

He turned to the boy.

"That right?"

"Yes, sir."

Homer whistled. "That's all right," Homer said. "I didn't even see what you did."

"Hell, no. You weren't supposed to. If you could see it, I wouldn't have done it."

THE SECOND MATCH was just like the first. His daddy
had a Gee Dominic, a local Georgia strain that a lot of
handlers didn't like because the color wasn't high and
it looked a whole lot like a regular chicken.

That's how come it's a secret weapon, his daddy said.

He saw one cripple a hawk one time when it tried to
grab a chick in the yard. The cock would have killed it,
but the hawk got away.

"That's one thing about hawks," he said. "They're
swift in the flight, but not in the fight."

"That's because they got good sense," Homer said.

"About like you," his daddy said. "That's right, ain't
it, Homer? Good sense and no guts to speak of."

Homer didn't say anything, and his daddy laughed
and hit him on the shoulder to show he was kidding.
But he wasn't kidding. It didn't take the edge off it.

The boy glanced at the bird in his daddy's arms and
thought how much it looked like a hawk. It had yellow legs and a brownish yellow tinge to its feathers like
a hawk when it's flying and the sun gets up under its
wings and the light glances off the feathers and turns
them sort of golden.

The other bird was a cross Rattler. His daddy didn't
know what it was at first because it was heavyset in the

wings. Most Rattlers are light. They come in at about four, four and a half pounds. This one was a little more than that. It had blue legs, and that's why his daddy thought it was a cross between a Tartar and a Rattler, most probably.

The boy had heard about Rattlers, but he had never seen one in a fight. They beat their legs like they're rattling a drum, his daddy said. The boy thought he meant a rattlesnake—that's what they're named for. But his daddy said, No, it was a drum.

And that's just what that Rattler was doing. He was all over his daddy's bird, legs flying, gaffs flashing, beating on him as fast as a drummer beats on a drum with his sticks. They got hung up, and when they uncoupled, the Rattler turned and started running. The Gee Dominic was chasing after it. A man started booing and then another, and it looked like the referee was going to have to call it off because the Rattler was showing his colors. His daddy was disgusted with that. He was swearing and cursing when all of a sudden the Gee Dominic got the other bird penned up in a corner. The Rattler tried to climb over him, but the Gee Dominic got a gaff in and pulled the other bird down on the ground and got on top of him, rolling around with his spur in the Rattler's body. Then he jumped off and ran at the Rattler again, and the Rattler just lay there. His daddy's cock had one spur in and was trying to pull it loose, flapping his wings and kicking his one free foot in the dirt.

The referee called for a handle, and his daddy went up and ripped them apart, he was so mad. The other handler told him to watch it, that was too rough, he was tearing up his bird. And his daddy said he didn't give a shit—that was no gamecock, that was just a Goddamn chicken as far as he was concerned.

His daddy was so mad the boy thought he was going to hit the other handler. And the handler must have thought the same thing himself because he picked up his bird and left. His daddy went and scooped up his Gee Dominic and came over, his hands shaking, he was so mad at that other chicken for running like that. He couldn't stand it, and neither could most of the men in the bleachers, especially the ones that bet on him.

The referee said that fight was forfeited and announced that his daddy's bird was the winner.

"What happened?" Homer said, coming up with the money he got from the betting.

"Son of a bitch ran," his daddy said. "Didn't you see him?"

"I mean did he kill him? Is he dead?"

"Who gives a shit?" his daddy said. "Goddamn dunghill son of a bitch! I don't think my cock killed him, but the one that owns it probably will as soon as he gets to where you can't see him."

"How come?" Homer said.

His daddy looked at him.

He didn't say anything for a while, then he said, "Homer, I can't believe it. You're a dumb son of a bitch. You can't keep a cock like that. What the hell's the matter with you?"

Homer didn't say. He just looked at his daddy, and his daddy asked how much money he made.

The fight was over in less than three minutes, and Homer made three hundred and eighty-two dollars, not counting what he knocked down for himself.

BY THE THIRD MATCH the tension was building. There were four cockers out of the sixteen that had won both their previous matches. The field was narrowing. This next round it would narrow even more.

His daddy was fighting a Red this time. He had a lot of Claret in him and a lot of something else.

"That's another secret," his daddy said. "The secret of breeding and knowing when to let good enough alone and when to go forward."

The Red was a big bird, almost a shake. His daddy had to do a lot of trimming and feeding him on vitamins to get his weight down. The bird hadn't eaten in a couple of days. They gave him some water, and he pecked at it, looking for food.

"That's one thing I hate about chickens," his daddy said when he saw him do it. "They're all heart if you breed them right, but they ain't got a lick of sense."

"I saw one they taught how to dance," Homer said. "The Southeastern World Fair. They had a chicken in a box. You put in a dime like a pinball machine, the music came on, and the chicken started dancing."

"I saw that," his daddy said. "They had it wired."

Homer looked disappointed.

"What you mean wired?"

"The floor of the box—they had it wired. You put in the dime, it turned on a heater, the floor got hot, and the chicken started lifting its feet to keep them from burning—and they called it dancing."

"Well, I'll be damned," Homer said.

"You're getting a real education," his daddy said.

"Seems like it," Homer said. "Ever since I got out of Detox, things have been happening."

"They happened before," his daddy said. "You just didn't notice."

"I noticed," Homer said. "They just didn't happen. Not like this. Not like they been happening lately."

"Well, I'm not going to argue about it," his daddy said. "I got this here cock to fight."

And he went off and fought it.

THE FIGHT lasted three or four minutes. The referee was just about to move it out to one of the drag pits when the other cock started running. He hit the fence and tried to climb up it. His daddy's cock was on him as soon as he hit the wire and got his gaffs in and hung up, they were so deep. The referee yelled, "Handle!" And the handlers came and separated them.

The other handler picked up his cock and said, "He's rattled," and held the cock up to the referee as though he ought to do something about it. Then he took the bird over to the boy's daddy.

"Listen to that," the handler said. "He's rattled."

"Goddamn right," his daddy said. "He ought to be. I hate a coward."

"He took a lot of steel," the handler said.

"That don't matter. He cut and run."

"What's rattled?" Homer asked the boy.

"The way he sounds," the boy said.

"I don't hear it."

"You're too far away. Daddy says when they get rattled, it sounds like a coffee pot perking inside."

"Is that right?" Homer said. "Wonder what does it."

"Blood in the lungs."

"Goddamn!"

"They get a hole in it like a balloon, Daddy says, and the air lets out, and it fills up with blood, and that's what you hear rattling in there. You hear them breathing."

"You ever hear it?"

"Not yet. I might if they get over here with it."

"Why don't they just suck it out?"

"What?"

"The blood."

"The lung'd collapse."

"Oh shit," Homer said. "I don't mind watching and betting on them, but I don't want to know what they're doing."

The boy looked at him.

"Not me," he said. "I want to know all about it."

"That's because you're going to be a cocker," Homer said. "You got to know. You don't have any choice in the matter."

"That's right," the boy said.

He felt grateful he had his daddy and not somebody like Homer to teach him.

Homer's all right, his daddy said, but he don't know shit about nothing except getting drunk, and it don't take much talent for that. Not to mention getting in trouble. I forgot about that. That's his main job, ain't it, Lily?

And his momma would start crying, thinking about how sad it was and how much she loved Homer in spite of himself.

And his daddy would say, Don't waste it, Lily. You're wasting a lot of tears on a drunk.

The referee yelled, "Pit them!" and his daddy and the other handler took their cocks to the center score lines and set them loose, and the cocks hit one last time, and that was it. The other cock just lay there, and his daddy's got on top of him and started pecking his head, trying to get at his eyes.

"That's enough," the other handler said and pushed the Red off.

"You giving up?" his daddy said.

"I don't need to. That cock is dead."

"Get it out, then," the referee said, "and let's get going."

They cleared the pit and went on with the round, and by the time it had ended there were two entrants left undefeated—his daddy and a cocker from Ocoee, Tennessee. A little while later the man at the mike announced the last and final round. He told all about his daddy and the name of his farm and the name of the man from Tennessee and his farm and how the next round was shakes, and being as how they were outsized anyway, both parties agreed to match them up and let that match determine the derby. A couple of people yelled something, but most of them didn't seem to hear what the man at the mike said. They just went about their business despite the glory about to descend on them. The boy couldn't believe it.

"Tell about my boy," his daddy yelled.

He turned to the boy and winked at him.

"Listen to this."

"That's right," the man at the mike said. "The handler for Snake Nation Farm in this round is the owner's son. He ain't but twelve years old, and this is the first cock he ever handled."

Then he told the boy's name and all about Lion and how the bird already made four thousand dollars and was fixing to make a little more if he was able to win this one.

"Able, hell," his daddy yelled. "He's already done it."

That got them to laughing, and the man on the mike said, "Go get yourself a little refreshment or let out some of what you took in already. The big show's about to commence. You all get your money ready. This is the main event of the day."

"Come on," his daddy said. "Let's go."

"You stay here," he said to Homer. "See what you can do about betting."

When they got to the cockhouse, the boy reached in with one hand and took the cock out in a handle. Then he held him to his chest like a puppy. He blew on his ruff. The feathers lifted and fell back in place again. The bird cocked his head and looked at him.

"Leave him alone," his daddy said. "He's got enough to think about without you messing with him like that."

"He isn't thinking," the boy said.

It was like a pool of darkness. The boy imagined the water at the bottom of a well. Whatever Lion was thinking was like that.

"I don't give a shit what he's doing. Leave him alone. I told you, Goddamn it, that ain't a chicken. He's a Goddamn wild animal. Now tie on the gaffs."

The boy took the special green waxed thread and tied on the gaffs according to his daddy's instructions, pausing every now and then to reset the angle.

"That's good," his daddy said, inspecting the tie when he got through. "Now here's what we do. We're matched up to the other winner. You know what that means."

The boy thought he did, but he wasn't certain. He didn't want to say one way or the other for fear he'd be wrong. He finally figured he'd better say something, so he said, "No, sir," and waited for his daddy to instruct him.

"It means it can't be a tie, that's what it means. That's kind of unusual, but that son of a bitch from Tennessee said that's how he wanted to do, and they asked me, and I said all right. I wasn't fighting it any- way, I said. And besides that it ain't my bird. I told them it was all right with you. That right?"

"Yes, sir."

"I figured it was," his daddy said. "That's how we'll do then."

The boy was still holding the bird. Suddenly, it struck fast as a snake at one of the buttons on his daddy's shirt under the unzipped coveralls.

"Look at that son of a bitch," his daddy said, admiring Lion.

He ran his rough hand down the bird's back, across the saddle.

The boy's heart filled with pride. His daddy might have been stroking his own head, he felt so proud. The main reason he had gone out all those nights in the cold and the dark to sit beside Lion was to get what Lion had, to feel it shift out of the cock and into him the same way a battery is charged with a charger until it was not only a part of him now, it was like the whole thing. He had all that power in him. The cock was like the root of his root, the knot in the ropes that tied him together, the source of all his unborn rage and hatred and pride and violence and joy and happiness and incomprehensible release—incomprehensible because it could be expressed only by and through the cocks he tended and hoped someday to fight, and by no other means. Whatever he felt was locked up inside him—inarticulate, unable to be pronounced as a stone is unable to be pronounced—the cock said it for him. When he heard Lion crowing, it was like something he had never known was in him before lifting its voice. He was able to pick it out from ten other cocks all crowing at the same time. It was like hearing his own voice coming back at him from another world. When he saw Lion fight, it was like seeing his own soul go forth from his body in ecstasy.

"You handle him right, there's no way this bird can lose," his daddy said.

The boy was suddenly afraid.

"Maybe you better handle it," he said.

"No way. I told you he's yours. I gave him to you, and I'm not going to take him back. I got a lot riding on this. Young son of a bitch like you—you'll steal their hearts. They'll look at you and think of themselves when they were just starting and bet their hearts out. Besides, this bird's a three-time champion. There's no way he can lose. Your momma could handle him and win. You ready?"

The boy looked at him and nodded his head. He felt his heart surge. His daddy believed in him, and he wasn't ever wrong about something like that. Not about him. Not about cocks.

"All right then," his daddy said. "Let's go."

- FIVE -

THE HANDLER from Tennessee was about fifty-five years old. He had on a pair of snakeskin cowboy boots with big heels and pointy toes with brass caps and, despite the cold, a straw hat with a sprig of cock feathers stuck in the band. He had on a black nylon jacket that was unzipped, and his belly stuck out like a rock he was carrying or like something vital that had slipped down from his chest and settled somewhere below his belt inside his trousers. It was hard and round and gray under his T-shirt. He had a cock slung under his right arm and was talking to the referee.

"There he is," his daddy said.

He started to leave.

"I'll be over there."

The boy was alarmed.

"Where are you going?"

"Over there."

He jerked his head back toward the bleachers.

"I got a lot of bets to get on with. You know what to do. That's a good cock. There's no way you're going to lose. Just stay up with him and help him out like I taught you, and he'll do the rest. I got to set up a few side bets, help Homer out. There're going to be a lot of people betting on you, son. Don't let them down."

He patted the boy on the back.

"I'm proud of you, boy."

"Yes, sir."

"Give him hell."

"Yes, sir."

He held the gate open, and the boy went into the pit.

The referee came over and took Lion and started to weigh him, but the Tennessee man said, "It don't matter. Let's get to fighting. I don't give a shit what it weighs. We already agreed to that."

The referee said, "That right?"

The boy didn't know or couldn't remember, he was so flustered, so he said, "Yes."

The referee said, "All right. You ready?"

The boy's lips were dry. He didn't trust them to say what he wanted, so he nodded his head.

The referee said, "Okay. Bill them up," and the two handlers moved forward to the near score lines in the center of the pit and rocked back and forth with their cocks in their arms so they could get a good look at each other. After a minute, the cocks were excited.

They were writhing their heads like snakes and struggling to get loose to kill each other.

"Okay," the referee said. "Let's pit them."

The handlers slipped their hands under the cocks in a handle and put the other hand on their backs, holding them upright. Then they moved back and bent over and set them down eight feet apart on the far score lines.

"Pit them!" the referee yelled.

The handlers let loose, and the cocks flew at each other like they were fired out of a barrel. They hit and went rolling over and over on top of each other. It was hard to tell where one left off and the other one started, especially with Lion and his two different colors. It looked like three or four of them out there spinning around like some kind of ball or wheel of feathers, kicking up dust. The pit had been sprinkled, but the cocks were stirring up so much dust that it was hard to see them. They hit the wire and bounced, and it knocked them apart, and they ran at one another again and got hung up with the gaffs in each other so deep they couldn't move. They just lay there on top of each other kicking their feet as though they were wired, trying to get up.

"Handle!" the referee yelled.

The boy went forward to untangle the birds. Lion was on the bottom. The boy couldn't tell where his gaffs were at the moment. He slipped his hands under the bird's body just as the Tennessee handler ripped his bird off. Both his gaffs were driven into Lion, one through the back of the head, the other through the neck at the shoulder. He wrenched the gaffs out, twisting them, making the wounds much worse than they had been.

"Hey! Don't do that!" the boy yelled, but it was too late.

"Do what?" the Tennessee man said, looking at the boy as though he didn't know what he was talking about.

"Tearing him up like that."

The referee came up.

"We don't allow no rough handling," he said.

"I know you don't," the Tennessee man said. "Tell him about it. I don't like messing with boys. I'd just as soon a woman handle that cock as a boy like that, bitching. I've been fighting cocks all my life."

"I know you have," the referee said. "You ready to pit them?"

They pitted them again, and again they hung up, and again the man ripped the gaffs out, twisting them, enlarging Lion's wounds. The boy was afraid to complain about it again for fear the referee wouldn't believe him. The man sounded so upset and angry the one time he accused him of it, the boy thought he must be imagining things. If it got bad enough, he figured the referee would do something about it. That's what he was supposed to be there for.

After the third handle, the boy glanced over at the bleachers. He caught his daddy's eye. He was drinking from a paper sack and gave him a thumbs-up. Then he went back to talking to a man in a duck billed cap that said Red Man Tobacco. Behind them, a couple of rows up, he saw a woman wrapped up in a quilt just like one they had at home. His momma called it Wild Geese because she said it looked like flights of wild geese, but the boy couldn't see it. Just like stars. She'd take him out in the yard at night and show him the constellations, but he never could see them. She saw bears and dippers and hunters and sisters and snakes and dogs, and all he saw were stars, just as in the quilt all he saw were squares of cloth cut in two and set in sideways running down it in rows like roofing shingles that the wind got up under and lifted. That's what he told her. That's what it looked like to him.

That's one of the main differences in a man and a woman, his daddy said. Women see all sorts of stuff like that. That's how come they make quilts and such.

"Tear him up!" Homer yelled.

The boy looked over. Homer was leaning on the rail at the side of the pit.

"Your daddy's got a lot of money on this, and I got a little. Don't let me lose it. I need all I can get, and then some."

He started laughing like it was a joke, but it wasn't funny. Nothing about this was funny.

"I won't," the boy said.

They pitted the cocks three or four more times. The scorekeeper called to the referee, and the referee came over and said, "We're going to clear the main pit."

"This is the main event in this derby," the Tennessee man said. "Let them fight it out in the main."

By this time Lion was in bad shape. The boy didn't know how bad because he didn't know about internal injuries, but he wasn't acting right to him. He called to Homer and told him to go get his daddy.

His daddy came over and said, "What's the matter? They going to let them fight it out here?"

"What's the matter with him?" the boy said.

"He's in shock, that's all. Blow on his back."

The boy blew on the cock's feathers as though he was blowing on a fire.

"Not like that," his daddy said. "Put your face in his feathers. Give him some heat."

The boy put his face inside the bird's ruff and opened his mouth and breathed his heat on the bird's skin. He smelled his own breath and the dry odor of feathers and the yeasty smell of malt. It tasted like metal in his mouth or the hot blood of a wild animal. He could feel the cock tremble in his hands as though it was still fighting or dreaming about it, the muscles quivering involuntarily as though they had electrodes embedded in them. The cock didn't know what had happened to him and probably didn't even know where he was.

Homer came up.

"What happened?"

"Goddamn cock," his daddy said. "Wore himself out killing that fucker."

"Look at the other one," Homer said.

At the far end of the pit the other cock was walking around pecking at cigarette butts and flakes of mica and straw. It might have been at home in the barnyard thinking about mounting a hen.

"It don't look wore out to me," Homer said. "You sure he's all right? I got a lot of money out on this."

"You got a lot of money out?" his daddy said. "Whose money you think it is?"

"Your money," Homer said. "I'm just taking an interest, that's all."

"Like shit," his daddy said.

He turned to the boy.

"Put his head in your mouth and blow."

The boy sat down and put the cock in his lap and cradled him with one arm and grabbed hold of his head with the other and put it in his mouth. The head had been punctured. The gaff had taken off part of the bill. Blood ran down from the wound at the top and dripped off the end of his beak like a jewel. A bead would drop, and another would swell and drop again. The boy could taste the blood in his mouth.

"Goddamn!" Homer said. "Looks like he's eating it."

"Not like that," his daddy said to the boy, pushing Homer aside. "You act like a woman. Let me do it."

He bent down and put the head of the cock in his mouth. He cupped the shaft of the bird's neck with his lips, then opened them a little and breathed. He kept it up for two or three minutes while the bird just lay there. When he got through, he spit out the blood and wiped his mouth with the back of his hand.

"That ought to do it," his daddy said. "Look at that son of a bitch."

The boy was amazed. The cock had revived so completely it was hard to believe that he had not come back from the dead. Even the blood on his bill had stopped running. The other wounds were so deep that the bleeding was all internal. Very little showed on the outside. It took a great deal of searching and fluffing of feathers even to find where it had been gaffed.

"I count ten," his daddy said, inspecting the cock carefully. "No, there's another, and another one here," ruffling the feathers on his right haunch. "He took a lot of steel, all right, but he's okay. It ain't hit nothing vital yet."

"Hell, yeah!" Homer said, getting excited. "It ain't even bleeding, and that stopped."

"Oh shit," his daddy said, ruffling the feathers on the bird's head. "Look at this."

The boy looked, but he couldn't see anything. He didn't know what his daddy was talking about.

"What is it?" he said.

Homer came crowding in to take a look.

"Nothing there," Homer said after he satisfied himself. "I don't see a Goddamn thing."

"White head," his daddy said. "This chicken's Goddamn head is white."

"What's the matter with that?" Homer said. "What's you mean white?"

"The skin on his head. Look there."

He ruffled the feathers with his thick thumb, and the boy could see the white, pimply skin and the feathers stuck in it like splinters of wood.

The boy thought of his own hair. His hair was black, and it parted like that. The skin underneath it was white. The part ran down his head like a scar.

"So it's white," Homer said, waiting for the explanation. "What the hell you expect it to be?"

"A white-headed chicken's no damn good."

"How come?"

"Don't ask me. I'm no doctor. Something's wrong with them makes them like that. They can't fight. They ain't got any lead in their pencils, that's what's the matter."

He turned to the boy.

"How long's he been like that?"

"I don't know. Just now, I reckon."

"Just now, hell. He's been that way. It don't just come on all of a sudden. It takes a while. What the hell I got you for?"

The boy didn't know. He was remembering when he was three or four years old—they went to a lake, and he walked out in the water and kept on going until all of a sudden it was over his head, and he tried to breathe, but it was all water, and he started choking and tried to get back, but he didn't know which way to go, he was so scared, and if somebody hadn't pulled him out, he would have drowned.

He was in over his head again now, it seemed to him.

It did not occur to him that his daddy might have been partly to blame any more than it did to his daddy. The boy's job was to tend the cocks and put them on the keep and get them ready for the derby according to his daddy's instructions. The fact that the boy was just a boy and never heard of the white head was no excuse. He accepted that without even having to speak of it or call it in question, and his daddy did too. The boy was to blame. Who else was there? The cock couldn't help it.

He gave the bird back to the boy.

"Go on and fight him," he said.

"What's going to happen?"

"He's going to lose. He's got the white head. I never heard of one like that winning."

"What do I do?"

"The best you can. That's all you can do."

"They going to kill him?"

"Damn right, they're going to kill him—a Goddamn, fucking champion bird."

He turned to Homer.

"How much you bet?"

"A hundred thirty-eight," Homer said.

"I got out a hundred and sixty, and some of that's bad odds."

"Me too," Homer said.

"I'm going to lose a lot of money."

He stared off at something across the pit, the way the cock used to do, seeing something the boy couldn't even imagine, and the boy held the bird in his arms. A white head. It was like being struck down with cancer before you were even old enough to know what it was and dying before you even grew up.

"Well, that's it," his daddy said. "There's no help for it. People and cocks are a lot alike in a lot of different ways, and dying's one of them. I don't care how game they are, it's going to happen sooner or later, and the best thing to do is to go off and leave them and get on with the rest of your life. I'm going back up there. There're some folks I was with," and he turned and went back to the bleachers.

"I'll fight him for you," the boy said, calling after him. "He's going to win. I'm going to make him."

His daddy lifted his arm and waved without even looking back. He just kept on going.

"You want me to help?" Homer asked.

"What can you do?"

"I don't know," Homer said. "I thought you might tell me."

"There's nothing *to* do. You heard what he said. It already happened. I should have done something about it before. It's too late now."

"You never can tell," Homer said. "Look at it looking."

The cock had his head up and was peering about, ducking it this way and that.

"Looks spry to me," Homer said. "Looks like you all fixed him up, blowing on him."

The boy nodded his head, and the cock nodded his, seeing the motion or sensing a shadow come over him.

Homer laughed.

"Looks like he just noticed you're holding him, don't he?"

The cock was reared back, inspecting the boy and looking aghast at the situation he seemed to find himself in.

"They ain't got a lick of sense," the boy said, quoting his father.

"I know that," Homer said. "I never did know what you all were carrying on about anyway. Chickens are chickens, no matter if you bet on them or not. Betting doesn't change a thing."

"They ain't chickens," the boy said, speaking now out of his own sure knowledge. "These got heart. These are game. These are what you call game fowl. A cock's the only animal God ever made that's steadfast," he said, remembering now what his father told him.

"That and a lion."

Saying that, the boy was reminded of why he wanted to call the cock Lion until his daddy said they don't have names. But he called him that anyway in his own heart. That's how it was, heart to heart—his heart to Lion's. His daddy didn't know a thing about it.

"The Bible says that," the boy told Homer. "Look it up for yourself."

But he wasn't certain if it did or not. His daddy didn't know a whole lot about what's in the Bible, but he acted like he did, and the boy even suspected he made things up sometimes and said he read about them in the Bible because he thought that gave them extra weight with some folks, and he was always glad to oblige them.

Lots of folks believe in the Bible don't know a thing about it, he said.

His momma would know, but he was afraid to ask her for fear his daddy was lying about it. The only thing he ever heard his momma say about cocks in the Bible is how one was crowing its heart out when Peter denied the Lord three times.

And he's been denying Him ever since, she said. Every time there's a cockfight or a derby.

"I don't doubt it," Homer said. "The Bible says a lot of shit like that. That's what's wrong with it, to my way of thinking."

The boy was surprised. He never heard anyone say that before.

"There's nothing wrong with the Bible," he said.

The words hardly fit in his mouth, he was so surprised at what he was saying.

"What's wrong is some of the people that read it."

"I reckon so," Homer said. "Keep it locked up so folks can't get at it, you won't have to listen to shit like that."

"Like what?"

"All that steadfast shit and such."

"It's God's way," the boy said piously. "He made two animals like that—the cock's one, and the lion's the other."

"So is a man," Homer said.

"A man ain't an animal."

"Well, I ain't going to argue the point," Homer said, and then went on about it some more.

The boy wasn't listening. He was thinking about the story in the Bible about the man who gave his servants some money called talents and told them to go make use of it, and the unprofitable ones hid theirs in the ground for fear they might lose it, but the good and faithful servants went out and put theirs at risk and made money on it and returned it to their master at the end of the day increased tenfold. And the boy took heart. Everything he had in him was put out at risk, just like it said to do in the Bible.

The cock was struggling to get loose. He felt the sinews and muscles thrust in his arms.

"He might not lose," the boy said.

"That's right," Homer said.

He reached out and touched the boy's arm.

"Your daddy's been known to be wrong before."

Not in the boy's experience. He felt his heart fail as soon as he heard Homer say it.

"Shit fire!" Homer said with a flare of false enthusiasm. "He's been known to be wrong about me. How are we going to fight this cock?"

"Wait till they tell us. There he is."

A man stepped into the pit and walked over to Homer.

"You ready to pit them?"

"It's my cock," the boy said. "I'm the one handling him."

"Who's this?"

"My uncle."

"Okay. Get him out."

"I'll be right over here," Homer said, leaving the pit. He grinned at the boy.

"Just call if you need me."

The boy was feeling too bad to grin back. He was glad Homer was there at the rail instead of sitting up in the bleachers carrying on like his daddy. But the confidence he felt a minute ago had drained out of him like the strength or blood or whatever it was in a white-headed chicken. The referee was over on the other side of the pit, talking to the handler from Tennessee. The boy watched as the man ran his cock into a corner, and scooped him up under his arm and carried him to the first score line. There were two of them, one for each cock, located twenty-two inches apart. That way the cocks were close enough. The handlers didn't have to bill them. They'd already been fighting, and their blood was up. They would go right to it.

The boy moved forward to get into position.

"You ready?" the referee said.

"Shit yeah," the man said. "I been ready, ain't you?"

The boy nodded.

"Okay," the referee said. "Pit them!"

And they released the birds.

The cocks fought for two or three minutes, and it was just the same as before. They kept getting hung up. The referee would call "Handle!" and the man from Tennessee would work the gaffs in deeper and then twist them out, injuring Lion each time he did it. The boy kept waiting for the referee to do something about it, but he acted as though he didn't even see it. One time the boy called him on it, and the referee told him to fight his cock and leave the refereeing to him. He'd call it when he saw a rough handle.

After a while both cocks were getting worn out. Sometimes they just lay there in a heap and rested on top of each other, panting. Then the Tennessee man's cock would get up and start pecking Lion, tearing at his comb and the feathers on the top of his head. He just about picked him bald. His comb was bleeding, and he just lay there. He couldn't get up. He didn't seem to have the strength. It looked as though he gave all he had, and then he didn't have any more. He gave out.

The other cock was standing on Lion, pecking at him, when the referee came over and said, "Well, what do you want to do?"

The boy didn't know what he meant.

"You want to concede?" the referee said.

The boy still didn't know what he meant.

"You want to give up?"

The boy was surprised. It had never occurred to him that that was an option. But as soon as the referee mentioned it, his heart surged, and he knew that was it. That was exactly what he wanted to do. Lion wouldn't have to die after all. He'd take him home and nurse him back to health again. His daddy would know how. He knew all about it. He'd give him some kind of medicine and cure the white head, and the cock would be just as good as ever. Maybe better.

"Go get my daddy," the boy yelled to Homer.

"What for?"

"Tell him I need him."

"I'm going to have to put the count on him," the referee said. "That bird's worn out."

"Wait for my daddy."

"I can't wait. That Tennessee son of a bitch is going to start thinking about what he's doing instead of scratching his balls and grinning about how much money he's making and call for a count any time now."

"I know he is," the boy said.

Just about that time his daddy came up.

"What's going on here?" his daddy said.

The boy explained what the referee said *conceded* meant. He didn't know if his daddy knew. It wasn't something he ever did and wasn't likely to know about.

"Hell, no!" his daddy said. "Fight it out. I don't give up."

Homer said, "That's you. That ain't the chicken. It's wore out. Why not let the boy have it?"

"Hell, no!" his daddy said. "White-headed son of a bitch!"

He turned to the referee.

"Get on with it."

"That what you want to do?" the referee said to the boy.

"What the hell you asking him for?" his daddy said. "That's my son. I'm the owner. I already told you what to do."

"He's the handler of record," the referee said.

"How about it?" he said to the boy.

The boy looked toward his daddy, but he wasn't there. He had already turned his back and was walking away.

"Keep him," Homer said to the boy. "Don't let them kill him. You got a dog?"

The boy shook his head no.

"Go on and keep it then. Chickens make good pets. Follow you wherever you go, if you let them."

The boy looked at the referee.

"Fight it out," the boy said.

"Okay," the referee said.

Just then the Tennessee man quit scratching his balls and called for a count, just as the referee said he would.

"They ain't doing anything but laying there," the Tennessee man said. "You sure that other cock ain't dead?"

The referee counted to ten, then ordered the cocks pitted again. The boy did what his daddy showed him. He breathed into Lion's back to warm the chill he got from the shock. He sprinkled water on his head and breathed in his bill. The bird looked traumatized or exhausted. His eyes were glazed and unable to focus. They kept drooping shut. The referee ordered the handle, and when the boy released the bird at the near score line, he just stood there. The other cock leaped up and gaffed him. Lion went down, and the other cock kept leaping on him, gaffing him and pecking his comb and the blood that ran down in his eyes. The Tennessee man called for a second count, but the referee said there wasn't any need to do that. Lion was dead.

They let the cock gaff him some more until the boy told them to stop. He was dead, wasn't he? What's the sense in doing like that?

"Let him come down," the referee said. "Let him enjoy himself a little. It's part of his nature. I'd have done the same for you."

Then he got hung up again.

The referee turned to the man.

"Go get him," he said.

The Tennessee man went over and got his cock, ripping them apart for the last time. The boy waited until he was done, then went over and picked Lion up by the legs and carried him out upside down so he wouldn't get the blood on his trousers. He was looking for his daddy. Homer went with him, saying things he thought would console him.

- SIX -

"WHAT THE HELL you got there?" his daddy said when he saw them come up.

"What you do with it?" the boy said.

He thought they might want to bury it somewhere.

"Throw it over there till they finish," his daddy said, and he indicated a corner of the building behind the bleachers. "They still got a bunch of matches. They'll get it later."

"Unless you want it," he said to Roma. They were wrapped up together in the same quilt by that time. "You want you some cock?"

Roma laughed.

"Not no dead cock," she said. "I had enough of that to last me a lifetime already."

She started laughing.

"We'll have to get you a live one, then," his daddy said.

"You might have to," Roma said. "It's been a long time if you do."

She laughed again and cut her eyes at him.

"Come on," Homer said to the boy. "We better leave before they get it on right here."

Roma laughed.

His daddy said, "We're just carrying on. You hear that, Homer? You know what I mean?"

"Homer gets carried away sometimes," he explained to the women.

"I bet he does," Janelle said. "He looks awful jealous."

"Go on," Homer said to the boy. "I got a lot of bets to pay out."

"I bet you do," Roma said. "You anything like this one here"—patting his daddy's leg under the quilt—"you probably put out a lot."

Then she started laughing again. She seemed surprised and amused at her boldness.

"Not me," his daddy said. "The woman puts out. The man bets, and the woman puts out."

"That's what I mean!" Roma shrieked. "Look at that."

She pointed down at the pit.

A new set of cocks from another derby were crashing into the wire and rolling around in the dirt like wheels. It reminded the boy of the throne of God and the eyes on it, spinning. One of the handlers was standing there watching, leaning up against the wire, scratching his balls as idly as someone else might scratch the back of his head.

"That's how they do," Roma said. "It's like there's a direct connection between them."

"You and your direct connections," Janelle said.

"If I had balls, I sure wouldn't scratch them."

"What would you do with them?" his daddy said.

But Roma wasn't paying him any attention. She was still looking down at the pit. One cock in the near drag pit was lying on top of another, not moving. The one on the bottom looked to be blinded, his head was so bloody, and the other was too tired to get in a gaff.

"How long they been in there?" Roma asked.

"I didn't see," Janelle said. "I wasn't looking."

"You'd think they'd get tired of doing them like that," Roma said. "Same old thing, over and over."

"They ain't like that," Janelle said. "They don't get tired in bed, do they?"

"Who does?" his daddy said. "That's only natural."

"You don't know Daryl!" Roma said.

She squealed, and they all started laughing.

The boy didn't see how his daddy could stand it, considering what had happened. He stayed a while, and when he didn't know what else to do, he took the cock to where his daddy had said and laid him down and stood there by him thinking about what he could have done. A few minutes later Homer came up.

"That's a lot of money," Homer said. "And I don't mean just what I bet. That's enough, but Goddamn, your daddy bet too. He must have lost five hundred dollars, not to mention the hundred dollars he paid to get into the derby and what he expected to make on it if he won. That's twelve hundred dollars right there. I bet he lost two thousand dollars, all told—maybe more. That's an awful lot of money."

But the boy wasn't thinking about money. He didn't even know what it meant. That was the first time he handled a cock, and it wasn't supposed to be like that. The Tennessee man cheated on him, and no one knew except him and the boy, and the boy felt guilty about it. He was weak and ineffectual. He didn't know how to make the man stop. If he was a man, he'd have known what to do. As it was, he felt as though he let Lion down, not to mention his daddy and Homer—and himself. He let himself down. But what was he supposed to do? The cock had a white head, and he didn't even know what it meant. Something was wrong— That's all he knew. Something was wrong, and the way he was feeling, it wasn't ever going to get better. It would be wrong for the rest of his life. Something went out of him when that bird died. It wasn't just Lion. It was something in him too. Lion was a real champion. He had let down the champion bird. The whole thing had been arranged—he was bound to win. And then all of a sudden he wasn't. Nothing happened like it was supposed to.

He tasted something in his mouth that wasn't his own spit and wasn't the taste of chicken blood either. It tasted like dirt when he had to eat it one time at school when another boy beat him up and held him down and scooped dirt in his mouth and made him eat it. It wasn't like cotton from running too much. It was gritty and dead like dirt. It was filling him up inside like dirt somebody poured in a bottle. When he got filled up, he'd be dead. This was the start of something that would go on for the rest of his life—like Homer. He never knew that before. He felt like grabbing the first person he saw—a young blond man with a thin moustache that looked like he drew it on with a pencil—and telling him it was an accident. He wasn't like Homer.

The boy never knew what an accident was or how tenuous life is, and now he knew, and it was as though the whole world and everything in it was full of mischances. That was the worst thing about it. Nothing seemed worthwhile to him. If it was like this—if everything was subject to blind chance and accidents—then what was the use? Why bother with anything? It would just be cut down. It didn't even make any sense. If he just knew why accidents occurred, that would be something anyway. But that's the whole thing about accidents. They don't make any sense. He might as well lie down and die himself as put up with accidents like that.

"Can't win them all," Homer said. "Look at me."

He slung his arm around the boy's neck and stuck his face in his.

The boy looked at him and then looked away. That was the trouble. He didn't want to be like Homer, getting drunk and going to Detox. He wanted to be like his daddy instead. It didn't seem to bother his daddy, the new knowledge the boy had acquired. His daddy was just like the boy was before it all happened. He didn't even know it was there. The boy wondered how he was ever going to get back to where he was before it all started.

"I'm going to go sit with my daddy," the boy said.

"Good idea."

Homer got up and went with him.

THE MAN in the duck-billed cap was gone, but the women were still there, sharing the quilt with his daddy and screaming and laughing. The boy sat down, and Homer crowded in next to him.

They were talking about strange pets. One had a dog that used to do tricks, except they weren't real tricks. Sitting up was a trick. So was shaking hands with a paw. The other one had a cat, and every time she went off and left it, the cat would go and pee on her pillow.

The boy quit listening after a while. Then they got talking about the differences between men and women, besides the obvious ones of a sexual nature.

"They don't know how to brush their teeth," Roma said. "You ever see what their toothbrushes look like? Not only that, their hands are hard."

"That ain't the only thing!" Janelle said.

They both screamed and started laughing.

"What else?" Janelle said when she got her breath back. "My mind's a blank."

"They got whiskers," Roma said. "And they like to kill things. Look at them cocks."

That sobered them up.

"They don't want to kill them," his daddy said. "They just want to win. They wouldn't be in it except for the glory."

"What glory?" Roma said.

"The glory of winning."

"That and gambling," Janelle said. "Daryl says a champion cock stands to make a whole lot of money."

"It ain't the money," his daddy said.

"That's right," Roma said. "It ain't the money, and it ain't the glory. It's all about cocks."

"Oh come on," Janelle said. "There ain't no difference between a man and a woman except what's hanging between their legs."

The boy kept looking over at his daddy, hoping he'd say something to him, but he didn't pay him any attention. He was grinning and laughing and acting like he was real pleased to be there. He didn't seem like a man who had just lost a couple of thousand dollars, not to mention a four-thousand-dollar cock and a son that had something happen to him he didn't even know what it was yet, except it was an accident and it wasn't even his fault. That's how it is with accidents. They're nobody's fault, they just happen, and you aren't ever the same again after that. They change you inside, and you never get back—not even if you wanted to. And not only that, you never forget it.

Except for his daddy.

He couldn't figure his daddy out. He saw what it was, just as the boy did, but it didn't seem to bother him. There were certain things the boy hadn't learned yet. That was the conclusion he came to. His daddy knew things he didn't even know about yet—secret things he hadn't told him. That's how come he didn't care. He knew how to handle it. The boy had just started handling things. If he was going to learn to be a good handler, he was going to have to stick with his daddy. Homer didn't know shit. That's how come he stayed with a boy instead of putting it behind him and having a high old time with women, like his daddy. Homer didn't know what else to do—that's why he stayed with a boy like him. He wasn't a man, except to look at. He was a drunk, his daddy said, and that made him disqualified.

His momma said, From what?

They were yelling, and the boy was in the bathroom and heard them.

The human race, his daddy said.

His momma said that didn't make any sense, and it didn't. It was like a lot of things his daddy said. He said them and worried about it later. Even he admitted that. That was another part of the secret. Do what you want, and let them sort it out.

"It's like they got a demon in them," Roma was saying.

Janelle agreed with her.

"They just want to tear things up," Roma said. "I got a nephew. He ain't but six years old, and he's already tearing things up. Give him a toy, that's how he does. He throws rocks at it or beats it with a piece of kindling. That's how he plays."

"That's right," Janelle said. "Daryl says he won't go to a dogfight. But roosters and cocks, it's a whole different matter."

"That's right," his daddy said. "It's part of their nature."

"I don't care," Janelle said. "I said, Daryl, I don't care. It's unnatural, making animals fight like that. And he said, It's more natural than playing baseball. A cock's part of nature. God makes it do it. Men just help."

"That's right," his daddy said.

"And I said, That's bullshit. That's bullshit, Daryl—and you know it!"

"That's right!" Roma said. "If we were doing it, we'd do it different."

"Do what?" Janelle said.

"Run the world."

His daddy laughed.

"Run the world!" Janelle said. "I wouldn't want to run the world."

"I wouldn't either!" Roma said.

"I wouldn't want to!"

"I wouldn't either!" Roma shouted, laughing at herself.

They went on like that, and after a while the duck-billed man came back and collected the women, and they went off shrieking and laughing and waving their hands.

THEY SAT THERE a while watching the cocks killing each other, and his daddy finally said, "Come on, let's go. I'm getting sick of this place, ain't you?"

Homer started to get up with him.

His daddy said, "Not you. Stay here if you want to."

"What do I want to stay here for?"

His daddy shrugged his shoulders.

"I thought you might drop me off," Homer said.

"How'd you get out here?"

"Somebody took me."

"Then somebody might want to take you back."

"They're already gone."

"Okay," his daddy said. "You ride in back with the chickens, you hear?"

Then he looked at the boy.

"Those that are left," he said. "Those that aren't dead already."

"He can ride in front with us," the boy said. "There's room."

"Not for me," his daddy said. "I don't want him crowding in. Unless you want to sit back there."

"I don't mind," the boy said.

"All right, then. Let's go."

They stepped down on the seats of the bleachers, steadying themselves on other people's shoulders, making their way by what looked like secret signals and hidden gestures until they were on the ground again. As they stood at the main pit, a pair of cocks smashed into the wire just about at the boy's head. He flinched and drew back.

His daddy laughed.

"They ain't going to get out," he said. "They ain't wild animals in a cage."

But the boy was not certain. He no longer knew who or where the animals were or where the cages began or ended. Something had happened. He did not know what it was yet exactly, but the cages had opened and something got loose and came out. He suspected it might be him. Or it might be his daddy. He wasn't certain. It might even have been something else he didn't even have a name for yet. The only thing he knew for certain was that it wasn't Lion.

Lion was dead.

AND THEN all of a sudden he saw him. It was as though he had risen from the dead and was coming out from under the bleachers at the far wall, stopping every now and then to peck at a feather or a piece of paper or a scrap of food just as he would have in a barnyard. It reminded the boy of chickens down at the Gold Kist processing plant in town. Every time he went with his momma and daddy to the Piggly Wiggly to get the groceries, there was usually at least one chicken on the side of the road outside the plant, pecking at scraps and pieces of trash or walking down the white line in the middle of the highway with cars zooming all around it.

His daddy always thought that was funny. He said he liked to see them out there. It was something he looked forward to.

His momma said, What for?

And his daddy said it gave him heart. It made him think he might even do like that himself. Seeing them chickens escape certain death gave him a little bit of hope.

And his momma said, No way. There was no way he was going to do like that, and she read from the Bible all about how short life is and full of sorrow. And that includes death at the end:

> There is hope of a tree, if it be cut down, that it
> will sprout again, and that the tender branch
> thereof will not cease. . . .
> But man dieth and wasteth away: yea, man giveth
> up the ghost, and where is he?
> As the waters fail from the sea, and the flood
> decayeth and drieth up: so man lieth down, and
> riseth not: till the heavens be no more, they shall
> not awake, nor be raised out of their sleep.

And his daddy laughed and said, Not for those chickens.

He used to pretend it was always the same one, and no harm ever came to it. It didn't ever freeze to death in the winter or get hit by a car or eaten by dogs or whatever could catch it.

That chicken's immortal, his daddy said. It lifts my spirit and gladdens my heart—like it says in the Bible —just to see it looking so healthy.

It was like that, seeing Lion walking around—only worse. The boy didn't know if the cock was real or not, at first. He was sure Lion was dead. The referee was sure. Everybody seemed to be sure. But there he was, walking around as though he might have lived there all his life. It was the first time the boy had seen Lion loose, and he was surprised to see how much it looked like a regular chicken. He had always seen his daddy's cocks either immobilized in cages or flying at each other in hatred and rage. He knew, of course, that they were just chickens. But he had not really believed it until that very minute. He thought they were larger and grander than that, bigger and certainly more fierce and wild. He stood there transfixed, looking at Lion making his way along the wall. Then he went over to get him.

"What the hell's that?" his daddy said.

The boy didn't answer. He went to the cock and stooped down beside it. He held out his hand, and the cock pecked at his thumbnail. He turned his hand over, and the cock pecked at his empty palm.

"That's that Goddamn chicken that's dead," his daddy said.

Homer said, "What chicken?"

"The one I lost all that money on. Look at him."

They went over to where the boy was squatting and watched as he reached out and picked up the bird. He held him in his arms like a puppy. Then he stood up and offered him to his daddy.

"What the hell's that for?"

The boy didn't know. He thought that he had failed them both, and he wanted to fix it somehow. He wanted his daddy to take the cock so he could make it well again. He'd know what to do. The bird was hurt, but he could fix him. He'd heal his wounds and fight him again, and it would be just like it always was, only better. He had been given a second chance. He could wipe out what happened today and start all over again when he was ready. He wasn't old enough for it yet, but someday he would be. He'd take care of the bird and do everything his daddy said and learn the real art of it, and someday he'd get to fight him again.

And this time he'd win.

"What the hell you think I want that for?" his daddy said.

The boy was confused.

"He ain't dead," the boy said.

"The hell he ain't."

"Don't look dead to me," Homer said.

"That's you," his daddy said. "Just because he's walking around don't mean he ain't dead."

"You could fix him," the boy said.

"What the hell I want to do that for? That cock's no good. Wring his neck, and let's get going."

"Let the boy keep him," Homer said. "They did real good. He might be able to fix him up."

"Listen here," his daddy said. "There're two things you don't know. One is he's probably bleeding inside. You don't know what's wrong with him. A cock takes a beating like that, he might live a day or two, but he's bound to die sooner or later."

He turned to the boy.

"No matter what you do for him, there're some things you just can't fix. You just got to take them as they are and go on about your business. That's the first rule about fighting cocks. It's a real sport, and the first rule of sport is be a good loser. My daddy taught that to me when I was your age, and it's one of the things I try to live by.

"The other thing about it is, even if he didn't die, he had all the spunk knocked out of him. A chicken that takes a beating like that isn't ever the same again. They're like Homer here. Ain't that right, Homer? They know what can happen to them. They lost their cherry, and they aren't ever going to do that again. They're too damn scared."

He punched Homer's arm to show he was teasing.

"They're about as tame as you are then—ain't they, Homer?"

"I ain't so tame," Homer said.

"Not when you're drinking. I'm not talking about when you're drinking. Drinking makes you crazy as hell. Whiskey puts a fire in you, all right. I mean when you ain't. I mean when you're walking around like regular folks, like you are right now. You're about like that chicken."

Then he turned on Homer and let loose.

"You stay out of my business, you hear? I tell that boy to get rid of that chicken, I tell him that for a good reason, and it's between him and me. I'm training him. He's my boy, and I'm going to raise him by myself without some son of a bitch like you sticking his Goddamn nose in my business."

"I know you are," Homer said, backing off.

"I got enough trouble with Lily without you butting in."

"I'm not butting in," Homer said. "I just don't see why you don't let the boy keep the bird. He could raise him like a pet. Chickens aren't so bad. You can't train them like a dog, but they'll come when you feed them, and you can watch them scratch in the dirt."

"I don't raise dunghills," his daddy said. "I'd just as soon kill them all if they turned into chickens. A boy of mine don't need a pet. He's too old for pets. I'm training him to be like me."

"Wring his neck," he said to the boy.

The boy said, "What?"

He couldn't believe it.

He heard what his daddy said, but he still couldn't believe it.

"Wring his neck. We got to go. They don't like them walking around like that. Take him back there"—he indicated the space behind the bleachers—"and wring his neck."

"Goddamn, Jake!" Homer said. "Back off a little. Let the boy keep it. What the hell's it matter to you? I'll pay you ten dollars. Here, take twenty," thrusting it at him.

"Go on, keep him," he said to the boy.

"I told you about that," his daddy said.

There was a strangled restraint in his voice that made him sound rattled. He might have been choking to death, trying to breathe his own blood. The boy knew the sound and had learned to fear it. His momma did too. Everybody who ever ran into his daddy and heard him like that learned to fear it at one time or another. His daddy'd get to sounding like that—choking the words—there was no telling what he might do. His daddy didn't know, and nobody else did either.

Homer must have known it too because he backed off as soon as he heard it.

"I don't mean to mess with your business," Homer said. "You know that. I was just talking. Seemed to me it wouldn't hurt."

He was waving his hand back and forth in front of his body as though he was trying to keep something from lighting on him.

"I know you weren't," his daddy said, calming down. "I just don't need you butting in, that's all. I get enough of that from Lily."

"I know you do."

"He's my boy."

"I know that, Jake."

"I'm going to raise him like I want."

"I know that. Lily already told me about that."

"I got a responsibility to him. Just like my daddy."

"I know that," Homer said. "You're right about that. There're different ways of seeing it, that's all."

"My way and yours."

"I don't mean that."

"I do."

He turned to the boy.

"Do like I said. I'm going to be right here watching you."

"Let me do it," Homer said. "There's no sense making him do it."

"It's his bird."

"All the more reason," Homer said. "He doesn't want to kill his own bird."

"Goddamn, Homer! He's got a responsibility to it. Just like a dog. Say you hit a dog in the road with your truck. It's your duty to kill it. You don't just drive off and leave it there. You do something about it. You cut it's neck. Whatever you have to. I even hit one with a shovel one time. That's all I had with me. You already bought it—that's what I figure. You hit it, you bought it. The boy fought that cock, and now it's dead, and he's got to kill it."

"Go on," he said to the boy. "Do like I said."

The boy still had the cock in his arms. He turned and went back to where the other dead birds were piled up waiting for someone to come and remove them. He stood there with his back to his daddy and buried his face in Lion's ruff one last time. He was too young to have had a woman and too old to sit on his momma's lap anymore, and his daddy was a man—he never touched him. So putting his face in Lion's ruff and smelling the odor of dust and feathers was as close as he'd ever got to being intimate with anyone or anything in the world. It was something there besides himself, like the smell of a lover's skin, and he went down into where it began and smelled the smell that rose out of it. Whenever he smelled that odor again, he would think of that moment. Then he put his hand on its neck and slung the bird around in front of him like something tied to the end of a rope. He made two or three circles with it, then flung it over into the corner. The bird hit the wall, bounced back, and kept on going, leaping and flailing and ramming itself into the corner. Then it turned and came hopping and rolling all over itself, coming right at him. The boy backed up as he would if a snake was trying to bite him. He was surprised at how much life the bird still had in it. It was as though something in it had built up and built up and was coming out now in hysterical, frenzied rushes and jerks. It had no direction. It went this way a while, then that. Then it rammed itself into the corner and kept trying to get through the wall. It climbed up the wall boards a little ways and then fell back on itself and climbed again. It did that two or three times, then fell and lay there twitching. The boy watched while the life drained out. When the bird was still, he went over and squatted beside it.

"Leave it alone," his daddy said. "They'll come and get it."

The boy ignored him. He put out his hand and touched the bird, cupping it with his open palm, as if to heal it or give it his warmth, and something went out of him when he did it. He could not have said what it was, but he felt something drain out of him. It was fast at first, then it slowed down and ran out through his fingers like the trickle of electricity flowing out of a charger, except it wasn't charging Lion. It was draining out of himself. Everything his momma taught him about the Bible and everything else drained out of him like oil draining out of a crankcase, until there wasn't anything left.

It was like believing in God and going out one morning to feed him and finding him dead and reaching out to put your hand on him, and he was still warm, but it was too late. You already killed him, and he wasn't ever coming back, no matter what the Bible said. He did it already. He had risen again from the body of death, and look what happened. He killed him again. Doing it one time wasn't enough. He had to do it a second time. That's what they meant by the Second Coming. Everyone that came back from the dead would not live again like the Bible promised. They would all rise up and die again. *That* was the promise.

It wasn't just Lion. It was all the nights he went out to be with him, feeling its spirit feed into his, filling him with the flinty seeds of light. The bird was both the promise and the fulfillment, the thing he himself would have turned into if he had been able to choose for himself and the thing he hoped someday to become just as his daddy had already become it. Now Lion had died, and all that was gone. All the boy's hopes and desires and dreams and plans for the future died along with him. And it wasn't just the bird and everything it had come to represent to him. It was his daddy and everything *he* had come to mean to him. That had died too when he ordered him to kill the only thing he had been given permission to love except for his momma, and she was a woman. It wasn't permitted to love her like that if he was going to be a man and not a baby all his life. But it ended up taking her too. It took away everything he ever loved and ever longed for and desired. And that's what his daddy had wanted to do. He had wanted to take everything else away from him and leave only himself in its place, and now he had even killed that too. The boy wasn't him. He wasn't his daddy and never would be. How could he be? He was just a boy. That's all that was left. He had thought that when it was all over, he would end up a man like his daddy, but now it was done, and all he ended up with was himself. And he couldn't bear that. No one could bear that, not even his daddy.

It would be years before he was old enough to know that was wrong, before he knew that that's all there is or ever will be because that's all we have—only ourselves—and so it has to be enough.

"All right," his daddy said, coming up. "That's enough of this shit. Let's get going. You're acting like a baby about it."

"Let him alone," Homer said. "The boy's grieving."

"I don't see what the hell for," his daddy said. "It's my cock. I'm the one lost all the money."

The boy looked up at him.

"I thought it was mine."

"It was in a way," his daddy said.

He looked at Homer as if he thought he might want to say something to help him out, but Homer was busy staring at something on the other side of the pit.

"I gave it to you," his daddy said, "but it was mine, else I couldn't have given it to you. That stands to reason."

"I thought it was mine."

"Of course it was yours. That's not what I mean. You fought it, you killed it, that makes it yours.

"I'd say he earned it. Don't you, Homer? I might have given it to him at first, but I'd say he earned it now, don't you?"

The boy's heart rose like a balloon until it was so high it lost all contact with the earth. There was just blue sky and air, it rose so high. It had been his bird. He had done what he had to. He hadn't failed him after all.

"That's right," Homer said. "That's what I'd say. Come on," he said to the boy, touching him on the arm. "You did enough damage for one day."

"What damage?" the boy said. "I did what I had to. It was my bird."

"That's right," his daddy said. "You couldn't help it. You're just a boy. You did what you had to, and that's all you could. Nobody's blaming you for that, least of all Homer. You never learned that, did you, Homer?"

"Learned what?"

"Like I said."

"I don't know what the hell you said."

"In that case it doesn't matter then does it? Come on," he said to the boy. "Your momma's waiting and worrying about you."

"Let her wait," the boy said. "Worrying is about the only thing I know she's good at."

His daddy laughed and hit his shoulder.

"Come on, you little shit," he said. "Quit talking like that about my wife."

The boy loved his daddy. That's why his heart soared like a balloon. He loved him more than he ever loved Lion. That's why he killed him—because his daddy told him to. He couldn't ever kill his daddy. If somebody told him to wring his neck, he couldn't do it. He loved him too much.

Then he thought about Lion. He hadn't thought he could do that either. He was confused. He didn't know what he was capable of doing or how he felt about himself or his daddy or Lion or God or his momma or who he used to be or who he'd become. All he knew was that something had happened. He didn't know what.

It would take a while to sort it all out.

THEY GOT TO THE TRUCK, and Homer said, "Here, you go sit up front with your daddy. I reckon you earned it."

The boy could see he was being polite. He didn't mean it. He expected him to refuse. But the boy was through with Homer. Homer was just like his daddy said. He couldn't have done what he just did. Neither could his momma. That was one part of it. One part of the puzzle slid into place. He might not know yet all that had happened, but he knew that much. None of them could have done what he did except his daddy. He was the one who had told him to do it. The boy figured he'd better stick close to him. He still had something in him the boy wanted. Besides that, they were alike—that was another piece of the puzzle that slipped into place. Pretty soon it would all come together bit by bit, and he would know what it was. All he knew now was what it wasn't. His daddy was the only clue. His momma was gone, and so was everything about her, including Homer. There wasn't much left but the cocks and his daddy and himself.

He had forgotten all about himself, not knowing exactly what that was. He wasn't his daddy, and he wasn't Lion. He was something else entirely different. The idea filled him with excitement, and he felt his heart soar again. He was going to find out. Someday soon he was going to find out what he was. He would grow to himself little by little just as he had grown to himself so far. Who would have ever thought he'd be what he already was? And look at him now. He was different from what he was just this morning. He was almost grown up.

He opened the door of the cab and got in and sat there waiting, content to be what he already was and what he was going to be when it happened and the whole thing was finally finished. They could take their time about it and do what they had to, just as he was doing. There was no hurry. All he had to do was live long enough, and it was bound to happen. He figured he could do that. In fact he figured he'd already done it. Whatever he had to do in his life, he had already done when he killed that bird. He still didn't know what that meant exactly, but he knew it was true the same way he knew his own name and answered to it. It was all true. Everything that happened to him was true. It was like being given a prophesy that already happened. It was already in him. He just hadn't caught up with it yet to know what it said or to be able to read it.

He heard his daddy say, "Get on in, Homer, and quit bitching and moaning about it. Move the cages away from the cab and sit back there. You won't be so cold."

He felt the truck shift as Homer climbed up in the bed. Then his daddy got in the cab, and they started home. The only empty traveling box was the one that held Lion, and the boy realized it didn't matter. He already had everything that bird had and more—everything he ever loved about him and more—otherwise he wouldn't have been able to kill him. It wasn't what his daddy said at all—that was another part of the puzzle. Whatever happened, it wasn't what his daddy thought, and it wasn't what Homer and his momma thought, it was what *he* thought, and he was going to figure out what that was in a minute. There was no hurry. Nobody could take it away from him because it wasn't something he *might* do. It was something he had already done. All he had to do now was figure out why he had done it and what it meant and what had happened to him when he did it.

THEY STOPPED at the square in front of the courthouse to drop Homer off. He was living in a room above the hardware store with a space heater and a little bathroom and sink. Until they had room for him in the Projects or until he got a job, either one. He was a stonemason, and he used to be a good one. He had a good eye for it. He was like an architect, envisioning the space and proportion, until his back gave out and he started drinking.

His daddy said he didn't know which one came first.

His momma said it was his back. The reason he drank was he couldn't work.

But his daddy said it was vice versa. The reason he didn't work was he was a drunk.

The boy didn't know what it was. He never knew Homer when he wasn't drinking or drying out.

His momma said, It wasn't the same man. If you knew him fifteen years ago, you wouldn't know him.

And his daddy said, Hell, he wouldn't know me. He wouldn't know you. Fifteen years is a damn long time.

And she said, It's longer for some than it is for others. For Homer it's been a long, long time.

And his daddy said, Since what?

And she said, Since he's been all right. You didn't know him.

I wouldn't want to, his daddy said. I already know him too good as it is.

"This is about it," his daddy said, stopping the truck and turning around to look out the back window.

He pointed with his finger and told Homer to get out. Homer climbed over the side of the truck and said something. His daddy rolled down the window and said, "What?"

"When do you want to do it again?" Homer said.

"Do what—lose money? I don't need you to help me do that. I can lose all the money I want by myself, and if I can't, this boy'll help me. He's real good at doing that."

"I thought you might want some help on the bets. I'm awful short."

"Call up Lily. She'll give you some."

"I thought maybe a few dollars now—"

"How much you make on the cocks that won?"

"Nothing. I bet it all on the boy."

His daddy laughed. "You dumb shit—here." He reared back in the seat and jammed his fist in the pocket of his coveralls. "Here's five dollars. That ought to do you. You're about in the same shape I am."

"I reckon so," Homer said.

"Wiped out."

"That's right."

"Well, I'll be seeing you. Give Lily a call. She likes to hear from you sometimes. I told her I don't know why the hell she should. It just costs me money."

He laughed to show he didn't mean it, but they both knew he did. Even the boy knew that.

"Next time we'll win," Homer said with all the assurance and apparent self-confidence of a drunk or a compulsive gambler.

"There ain't going to be no next time," his daddy said. "Not for me, not for a while. I spent my best cock. The other ones ain't worth a shit. I wouldn't bet on them. I don't have any confidence in them. I don't mind running them a little in derbies. But I'm not going to bet any money on them. I get me another champion sometime, I'll give you a call."

"Call me before then," Homer said politely, using the formulaic response. "I sure would like to know how you're doing."

"I'll do that," his daddy said, responding in the same fashion. "I'll see you later."

"I'll see you and raise you ten," Homer said, making a little joke out of it.

That's how he was, his daddy said. Always joking. And the jokes were always as sorry as he was.

And his momma said, He's just trying to get you to like him. Why are you so mean to him, Jake?

Homer turned to the boy.

"I'll see you, Sonny. Sorry about all that."

"Don't tell him that," his daddy said. "It ain't your fault."

"I know that. I'm just sorry it happened."

"I'm not," his daddy said. "Why should you?"

"What you mean, you're not?" Homer said.

"I put it behind me. Hell, it's gone. Get up and walk away from it, I say. There's no sense in trying to live back there. Ain't that right, boy?"

"Yes, sir. That's right."

"That's how we do, ain't it, boy?"

"Yes, sir."

"He's learning," his daddy said to Homer. "He's going to be all right in a while."

"He already is," Homer said, smiling at him.

"Not yet," his daddy said. "But I'm working on it. He's going to get better." He laughed and said, "Hell, the son of a bitch is bound to. He can't get much worse."

He rolled up the window, and Homer stepped back and waved. He was still waving when the boy and his daddy circled the square and headed back home. The boy imagined him still standing there all by himself on the empty square, waving like that the rest of his life.

- SEVEN -

As soon as they were out of sight, Homer crossed the square in front of the courthouse and went down an alley behind the Ace Hardware Store and Furniture Gallery on the corner. The alley was full of garbage cans and delivery trucks and rickety wooden steps leading up to second-story rooms over the stores. Some of the steps went up to a wooden gallery, others just went straight up to a door. Homer's had a gallery attached. If he was still there by the time it was summer, he could picture himself sitting out there, smoking a cigarette, talking to friends. Maybe even having a drink. He'd be dried out by then and probably working full time, maybe even working for Jake.

The stairs pierced the floor of the gallery, and Homer went up through the tunnel of wood and emerged as into another dimension. Once he was up on the floor of the gallery, he knew he was safe. It was partly the height, which gave him a sense of being lifted far above all human concerns. But it was also the total, cumulative effect of everything that ever happened to him. Often at night he would stand at the railing and look out over the town and see in the distance the lights of the houses twinkling far off across the valley and up the slopes of the dark, circling mountains. This is my place, he would think at those times. This is where I am. They are there. He was more alone than he wanted to be, but at the same time he considered it almost a blessing. He did not know the name for what he was feeling at moments like that—he thought of it as an edge or outrider of happiness just as false dawn is not real dawn but the illusion of dawn that gives a promise of what is to come. Compared to Detox and what went before, it was almost like peace.

He stood there a moment, looking out across the valley, feeling the distance between himself and the rest of the world. Then he went in and locked the door and made a hard salami sandwich on dry bread. He heated a can of Campbell's Tomato Soup and got out some soda crackers and a tin of Vienna sausages and a Coca-Cola. He proceeded to eat it all. Then he threw away the cans and paper plates and plastic utensils and lay down on the bed and thought about money before he turned to the actual pleasure of counting it.

He thought about all the things he might do with the money besides paying rent and buying groceries and new clothes to work in, if he ever got a job. He thought about how he might buy Lily's boy a pet—a dog or a cat, or even a chicken. Then he thought about Lily. He'd get her some flowers—long-stemmed roses—or a box of candy. And Jake might like a bottle of whiskey. Then he thought about whiskey a while until he figured he'd better quit. It was making him thirsty.

He rolled over and got out his wallet and noticed that he still had his shoes on. He was afraid they might have chicken shit on them. He looked, and they did—something, anyway, packed in the lugs. Maybe it wasn't chicken shit. He considered himself an optimist and figured maybe it was just mud. Or cow shit. He sat up on the side of the bed and took his shoes off and threw them across the room into the corner. He smelled the dark stains on the bed. He couldn't tell. It smelled like wet mattress to him. He lay back and bunched up a pillow under his head. Then he opened his wallet and counted his money.

Besides the nine dollars he had kept hidden away in a special compartment, he had a total of seventy-eight dollars. Eighty-three including the five dollars Jake just gave him. Counting the nine he already had, that made ninety-two. It wasn't his money, of course. Not in the sense that it was his to begin with. He made it by knocking down on Jake a little bit at a time and then in the end betting it all against the boy. It was the only bet he made all day. Even money. He made forty-five dollars on it. The rest he got out of Jake. Plus the five dollars, of course, which he figured was what Jake ought to have paid him. That and the pleasure of being there with him and helping the son of a bitch lose his money.

Homer never liked Jake any more than Jake liked him. They were two totally different people. Jake got along. He liked people, and they liked him. He liked having a good time and cheating on Lily and not thinking about it too much. But Homer never felt comfortable with him, or with anyone else for that matter. He only felt comfortable when he was drinking. That's why he drank. It was like having an itch all over, except it was in his head.

Thinking about not ever having a drink again was depressing. It was like losing a part of himself—the best part. The one that gave him the most satisfaction and led to what he considered to be his real self. Drinking was the key that opened the door, and when he finally got drunk enough, his real self came roaring out, like one of Jake's cocks, crowing for daylight and scratching his feet. He smiled to himself, thinking about it. That's what it felt like. And here he was—shit!—covered with almost a hundred dollars in bills.

He started thinking about all the people he knew who might like a hundred dollars to spend. He thought about his ex-wives, one of whom drank with him and one of whom didn't. The one that did would surely like to have it to spend. The other one would probably take it from him, if she knew he had it, and then want him to buy something useful with it. That's why he couldn't stand living with her—she wasn't much fun. And the reason he couldn't stay with the other one was that she was. She was a little too much fun. He loved them both in different ways. One was like Lily. She did what she could with a bad bargain. The other was more like him, and he couldn't stand himself too long, let alone somebody else just like him.

He thought about his children and tried to figure out how old they were now, but all he could remember was how old they were then, and even that was just bits and pieces like a series of photographs in an album. They were always the same age they were when he left them, or they left him, depending on which one of his wives it was.

That got him thinking about Lily's boy, and the more he thought about him, the sadder he got. He hadn't thought much about it before because he was too busy, but now he had time, it was real sad. The more he thought about it, the more it seemed like it happened to him. He used to always start off like that, with high hopes and great expectations. He'd try to do the best he could, but something like that would always happen, and he'd lose whatever it was he wanted, whatever he had hoped for or needed or loved. He didn't know why. Something was missing. It's like what he was wasn't enough. People like Jake got along. They knew how to do without even thinking. People like him, on the other hand, didn't. They weren't mean enough, for one thing. And they were always thinking about things too much. It was like he kept yearning for something. He didn't know what it was, but he could almost see it sometimes when he was drinking, and he kept thinking, If I could just get drunk enough. . . . But he never could. It was always just up the road, around the curve, in the far distance— some kind of integrity or completeness, some kind of fulfillment.

That proves there's a God, his daddy had said. You couldn't even imagine a thing like that if God didn't put it in your head. That's why you're so restless. He's calling you, son. He wants you to seek him.

But Homer didn't believe that. He believed in the need. He believed in the longing. He believed in the yearning and dissatisfaction. But he didn't believe in a God that would create that hollowness in him, full of emptiness and desire, just so he would seek Him to fill it, and not give him any sort of peace or rest or satisfaction in anything else until he did. It's like God wanted him to give up the whole world just so he could find some rest in Him.

The more he thought about it, the more depressed and restless he got until he was itching to get out of there. There was no telling what he might do if he stayed.

He took the money and put it back in his wallet. Then he went over and picked up his shoes and started to put them on when he stopped and took out his wallet again and counted out fifty-two dollars and hid it in the mattress—not at the head of the bed, but at the bottom, where he'd cut a slit with his knife. He slipped the money inside the mattress and patted the stuffing back in the slit and smoothed it out and put on his shoes and then his coat and went out on the gallery and looked at the stars. He looked at the distant lights twinkling on the side of the mountains. They looked like stars that had fallen down there on the edge of the sky. He imagined all the happy families doing what they did on TV and wondered why he was impaired and why he thought he had to have more than they did. They didn't need all that excitement. They didn't need to keep on finding themselves over and over and over again, always having to make a new start.

THE NIGHT WAS COLD, and he pulled the collar of his coat up around his ears and jammed his hands deep in his pockets. He rounded the corner of the alley and crossed the empty street to the square in front of the courthouse. At the far end was a public telephone on a post. It was painted light blue, with a plexiglass hood that reminded him of a hair dryer. The wind was blowing and bitter cold, and he squeezed up under the hood, glad for even that much shelter. He fished out a quarter and dialed the number and counted the rings. After five and a half, Andy came on.

"That you?" Andy said. "Where you been all day? I been trying to get you."

"Helping my brother-in-law."

"Doing what?"

"He had some business," Homer said evasively.

"What about the job?"

"I didn't go."

"You mean you didn't keep the appointment?"

Homer didn't want to say if he did or not, so he didn't answer.

"You call them or what?" Andy asked.

"Yeah."

He knew Andy would find out sooner or later, but he didn't want to deal with it now. He already had too much on his mind. Besides, he was so used to lying that it was simpler than telling the truth. Lies were easy. Truth was hard. The light of truth was a hard white light, but the light of lies was mostly all shadows.

Andy was a professional counselor at the Alcoholic Rehabilitation Center. He was dried up now, but because of his previous experience, sorely bought over thirty years of hard, steady drinking, he was regarded as an expert on the subject. Homer got two or three months of him through Mental Health after he got out of Detox. They called it being a sponsor.

"Listen," Homer said. "I got something important to tell you."

"I got something to tell you, too," Andy said. "I went to a hell of a lot of trouble—"

"Shut up and listen," Homer said.

"You been drinking?"

"Not yet—"

"What's the matter?"

"I don't know. Something happened, and I got to thinking—"

"Don't think!" Andy said, breaking in on him. "You get to thinking, first thing you know you're full of regrets."

"I know."

"Then you get drinking. You know what they say?"

"I know."

"Easy does it."

"Yeah, I know."

"One day at a time."

"I know."

"That's good. Listen, I got to go. I'm telling my story. It's my tenth anniversary. I got a cake and a special chip. You coming?"

"I don't know."

"Sounds like you better. You know what they say?"

"Yeah."

"Ninety meetings in ninety days, you get your first chip. It's the only way."

"Yeah," Homer said. "But I got this nephew, and he lost his cock."

"No shit!" Andy said. "How old was he?"

"Twelve or thirteen."

"Twelve or thirteen! Goddamn, that's awful! What was it, an accident?"

"It wasn't that kind of cock," Homer said.

There was a pause.

"What kind was it?"

"A chicken."

"A chicken!"

"Yeah," Homer said. "That ain't important, but it was his first, and his daddy lost a lot of money on it."

"Tough shit," Andy said. "It ain't your fault."

"Whose fault is it?"

"Nobody's fault. Things like that happen. There's a whole lot worse things than losing a chicken."

Then Andy started telling him about all the things he had lost when he was drinking—the good jobs and the wives and the innocent children and the boats and cars and furniture, not to mention his own self-respect. He had even set his own house on fire one time just to get the insurance.

So what? Homer thought. It seemed reasonable to him. You got a house and you need the money, it seemed to him like a good idea to set it on fire.

He knew what he should have done. He should have told Jake he was being a shit and then grabbed the chicken and killed it himself and given him the money for it. But he was afraid to. That's what really bothered him—that and the fact that the boy had to do it all by himself. He knew what it felt like—having to kill something you love. It never got easy, no matter how many times you did it. Whatever was going to happen to the boy from now on and whatever he was going to turn out to be was bound to be affected by what had just happened. The whole rest of his life was going to go spinning out of killing that cock, slinging it around by its head in a circle like a wheel of fire throwing off sparks in every direction.

But maybe not. What did he know? Maybe Jake was right after all. Homer didn't know how to do for himself, so how could he expect to know how to do for a boy, except to tell him it didn't matter when both of them knew in their hearts it did.

Andy was still going on about all the awful things he had done, and Homer was tired of hearing about it. It sounded like bragging.

"Listen," Homer said, breaking in. "You're going to miss your meeting."

"Oh shit!" Andy said. "I forgot all about it. You coming?"

"Yeah," Homer lied.

"That's good. You know what they say?"

"I know."

"Go to meetings and don't get drunk."

"I know."

It felt like a real physical pain in the center of his chest—some sort of knot somebody had tied before he was born, balling him up. It was too tight. That was the trouble. He was strung up too tight. The only way he knew how to get loose was having a drink.

But that wasn't it. That wasn't what he needed right now, he told himself, lying again. What he needed to do was to talk. He needed somebody to listen to him who wasn't getting paid for having to do it, and the only place he could think of was Harry's. There was always somebody there who wasn't hurrying off to a meeting to tell his life's story and get another chip for his birthday. Somebody there could listen all night. He didn't have to drink with them. He could have a bottle of Coke and some peanuts, the way he did when he was a boy. The innocence of it appealed to him, and he thought about Jake's boy again and how he regretted not doing for him what he knew in his heart he should have done.

As he hung up the phone and stepped out from under the plexiglass hood, the wind hit him and cut through the thin canvas shell of his coat. The only way to get there was walk, so he headed out through the square and down the street that turned into the Chatsworth Road. When the town ended and the sidewalk gave out, he walked on the shoulder of the road, facing the cars. The ground was rough, and he had a hard time keeping his footing. The shoulder dropped off sharply on his left, and he walked on the blacktop whenever he could until he saw the red neon sign shining like a beacon of hope far off in the darkness.

He dropped off the road onto the gravel parking lot surrounding the low, red brick building. There were a few cars and trucks parked near the door. The neon sign on top of the building was blinking on and off.

Harry's Package Store, it announced in the darkness.

Then it was gone.

Then it appeared again, casting its own strange light.

The gravel he walked on kept coming and going the same way. First it was a pool of blood, red and iridescent. Then it suddenly lost its color and turned into dirty gray rocks in the darkness. Then it flashed red again. He was glad to get inside, not only because he was cold, but because the light was oddly disturbing, especially when the gravel turned into blood.

He slammed the door after him and stomped his feet to get the circulation back, and Harry looked up from the bottle of beer he was opening for a blonde-headed woman sitting in front of him at the bar.

Homer checked out the rest of the room. Besides the woman at the bar, there were six or eight other people sitting in the shadows at tables. He couldn't tell and didn't much care. He wanted the bar. He wanted to talk and share the simple, unaffected comradery of just sitting there drinking, passing the time, talking to whoever happened to be there about whatever happened to come up in the course of regular, ordinary conversation.

Homer went over and sat on one of the bar stools not too far from the blonde-headed woman and not too close either. The bar stools were made out of chrome posts with rotating red vinyl seats on top. He sat down and twirled around in a circle, pushing himself off on the bar.

He did that a while, amusing himself. Then Harry came up.

"Long time no see," Harry said.

Homer quit spinning.

"Yeah. I been away for a while."

"Where you been?"

"Detox."

"I figured that must have been it. You were in bad shape last time I saw you."

"I know it," Homer said. "I wasn't feeling myself at all."

"What can I do you for?" Harry asked.

"A bottle of Coke and a bag of peanuts."

"You want something in it?"

"No, just the Coke."

"How about a glass?"

"The bottle'll be fine."

Harry hesitated a moment. Homer looked up.

Harry said, "That all?"

Homer said, "Yeah. I'll let you know later. Right now I'm still working on Detox. I can remember some things about it, and what I don't, I'd just as soon forget."

"I don't blame you," Harry said. "I'll be back in a minute."

Harry left, and Homer glanced at the woman beside him. He had never seen her before, but he could tell from looking at her that she probably wasn't too much of a talker. She was drinking what looked like but could not have been a Tom Collins. Homer glanced at it again, then at the woman. She was forty or fifty. It was hard to tell. Older than he was. She looked a little like Lana Turner with her hair pulled back in a bun the way Lana Turner did sometimes. She was so blonde it made her look skinned, but elegant too, in a hard looking way. Her eyes were bad. They were all pouchy, and the skin on her neck was getting wrinkled. He thought maybe that's why she pulled her hair back like that— to pull the wrinkles out of her face.

Harry brought him what he ordered and set it down and then went over and sat at one of the tables. Homer checked the woman out again in the mirror behind the bar. She caught him looking, and he glanced away, suddenly shy. He chugalugged a third of the Coca-Cola, then opened the bag of peanuts and poured them in the bottle. Then he put his thumb over the top and shook up the bottle until it was about to explode. Then he slid it over his mouth and released his thumb. His whole head exploded, and he almost drowned. His ear and nasal passages were full of Coca-Cola and peanuts, and some of it dribbled out of his mouth and down his neck into the collar of his shirt. He banged the bottle down on top of the bar while it was still erupting, spewing and fizzing and boiling over.

He was almost choking to death on the peanuts and had to spit some of them out in his hand. He chewed up the rest and washed them down with some more Coca-Cola. He glanced in the mirror and saw the woman looking at him with a disgusted look on her face.

He turned to her quizzically.

"What's the matter?"

"That's not the question," the woman said. "God, that's disgusting!"

Homer didn't even know what she meant. It seemed perfectly natural to him.

"We used to do that when I was a boy," Homer said.

"Well, shit!" the woman said. "Button it up."

Homer wondered what that meant.

"I don't do it with beer," he said.

The woman didn't even bother to answer.

"Just Coke."

He caught her eyes in the mirror and spoke to her there.

"What's that you're drinking?"

"None of your business."

She wasn't very friendly, Homer observed. She might have been too drunk to be friendly. It was hard to tell.

"You just get out of Detox?" he said.

"Of course not!"

She sounded insulted.

"I did," Homer said. "I thought maybe that's why."

"Why what?"

"Why you're drinking something like that."

"Because I like it," the woman said. "Because I was in England, and that's how they do."

"Drink Tom Collins all year?"

"You drink iced tea all year, don't you?"

Homer couldn't see the relationship, but that was all right with him. He had got her to talking.

"I might have me a beer," Homer said. "You want another?"

"Not me."

He caught Harry's attention and got a beer and chugalugged it, then got another and did the same. Then he asked for a shot of rye whiskey and washed it down with a chaser of beer. A boilermaker. He didn't know why they called it that. He had another, then another. Then he was off the ground and flying. The alcohol started flowing, his arms and legs filled out, then his chest and his head. His heart got bigger, and his brain was more active, and he started feeling real good.

"Looks like Detox agreed with you," Harry said.

"That's what everybody's been saying all day," Homer said.

He was feeling very benevolent. It wasn't so bad after all. It was all right, in fact.

"You been drinking all day?" Harry asked.

"No. Just now. They say it about eating. I've been eating ever since I got out of Detox."

"That's good," Harry said. "Eating's good for you. Quit eating, that's when you end up in Detox."

"Don't I know it," Homer said. "Give me another."

"You sure?"

"Damn right, I'm sure. I want to talk to this little lady."

The woman looked at him.

"I ain't got nothing to say," she said.

"I wouldn't doubt it," Homer said. "You look kind of sour."

"That's nice," the woman said. "That's real nice. That's a real compliment, that is. You know why I look like that? I got marital troubles, that's why. That's inclined to make you look sour."

"You married?" Homer asked.

He looked for a ring.

"I used to be," the woman said. "That's what's the trouble."

Homer was feeling too good to worry about that.

"Let me ask you something," he said. "What you think about a boy lost his cock?"

The woman looked at him suspiciously, but he wanted to see what she said.

"You got any opinions on that?"

"Lots of them," the woman said.

"Like what? Give me one of them."

"Tough shit," the woman said.

"What else?"

"Who gives a shit?"

"He does," Homer said, smiling. "If you had a cock, you'd know what it meant."

"Seems like I don't," the woman said. "I wasn't supplied one. In which case, I don't give a shit. I don't even know him. My former husband had a cock, and I know for a fact he would have been a whole lot better off if he didn't. And I would too. This way he'll probably be happy. So will the women."

"What women?"

"The ones he don't try to stick it into."

Homer whooped. That's how he was feeling.

"You act like you got a chip on your shoulder," Homer said. "You want me to knock it off?"

The woman said, "Yeah."

Homer suddenly realized that he wasn't sure he knew what she meant.

"You mean you want me to knock it off, or you want me to shut up?"

The woman said, "Both."

"You can't have both. It's one or the other."

The woman didn't even respond. She looked real pissed. But that was her way. He wasn't about to let it disturb him. A month in Detox made the present moment too rare. It was too precious to waste on feeling regretful or ill-tempered or arguing or fighting. It called for love. The more he sat and talked to her, the better she looked.

"What if told you it was a chicken?" Homer said.

The woman said, "What?"

Homer said, "His cock," and smiled.

She just looked at him.

"I've known some I wished they were," she said.

"I mean it," Homer said. "It made him real sad. It was a chicken, and it got killed, and he felt real sad about it."

"Well, shit," the woman said. "Get him another."

And suddenly he knew that was it. That's how he could fix it. He wondered why he didn't do it before. It was so simple.

"All right!" Homer said. "Where do I get one?"

"How the hell do I know?" the woman said. "Where'd he get the other one?"

"Hey, Harry!" Homer shouted.

He started moving as soon as his feet hit the floor. He lost his balance and had to steady himself on the bar. The floor tilted, and everything looked loose and unstable. He hung onto the bar and lowered his head until it quit swimming. Then he yelled for Harry again and started out to look for him.

They met in the middle of the room.

"Where can I get me a chicken?" Homer asked.

A man in the shadows started laughing.

Harry smiled and said, "Gold Kist. Down at the plant."

"Not that kind of chicken," Homer said. "I mean a cock."

"Fighting cock?" Harry asked.

"That's right."

"There're some cages down on the road. You passed right by them. What's his name?" he asked the men in the shadows. One of them told him who it was, and Harry said, "That's right."

He turned to Homer and told him the man's name.

"He raises them, but he doesn't fight them."

"They fight them in the Philippine Islands," one of the men in the shadows said. "That's where he ships them. Imagine that."

He sounded amazed.

"He might sell you one in the morning, you go by and ask him," Harry said.

Homer nodded his head and kept his own counsel. Morning was too late. He needed it now. He knew where it was. He remembered passing right by it. He'd pick one up on the way back and take it to Sonny.

"Thanks, Harry," Homer said, patting him on the shoulder. "You're a real pal."

"I know I am," Harry said. "I'm everybody's God-damn pal."

One of the men behind him laughed. It sounded like Jake. Homer tried to get a good look at him, but he couldn't see him.

He went over and sat on the stool by the woman.

"You want to help me?"

"Do what?"

"Get me a cock."

"You already got one," the woman said, suddenly smiling. She looked a whole lot better to him now than she did, except for her teeth, which were a little discolored and gappy. Even with that, she was still looking better.

"Damn right!" Homer said. "I ain't lost it yet. What do you think?"

"About what?"

"You and me joining forces."

"Doing what?"

"Looking for cock."

"That's what I'm doing!" the woman said and laughed at herself for being so forward.

Homer thought she was getting real friendly.

"You want another?"

"Don't mind if I do," the woman said.

AN HOUR LATER they were in her car. Homer was driving. She was sitting next to him, telling him where everything was on the car and feeling him up. He had turned on the heater, and it felt real good. They talked about where they would go—his place or hers—and they both started laughing because it seemed just like a movie.

"Better your place than mine," the woman said. "My car, your place."

"How come?" Homer said.

"I'm living with my brother," the woman said. "He sleeps awful light, and so does my momma."

"You live with your momma?"

"My brother does. I'm staying with him."

"My place it is, then," Homer said.

Ten minutes later they were in bed, their clothes strewn in a trail all the way from the front door to the bed—just like the movies. Everything they did was like in the movies.

HE WOKE UP about four o'clock in the morning and got out of bed and looked at the woman. She was still sleeping. The cold light of the moon fell on her face. Her mouth was open, and her hair was loose and scattered on the pillow like strands of seaweed. She was older than he thought. She looked drowned. He felt guilty, as though he had done it. He was sad for them both for being so desperate. She almost looked innocent, asleep.

The woman was sprawled on the bed, lying on her back. Her legs were spread, and he couldn't remember what they did or even if they did it or not. He thought of his sperm still warm in her body—if that's what happened. It seemed real strange—him here and her there and his sperm still inside her, maybe, still warm.

What's the use? he thought. What's the use in living like that? He didn't want to, but he was afraid not to. Pretty soon she'd wake up and go home, and he'd promise to see her, and maybe he would, maybe he wouldn't. Maybe he'd even marry her. It didn't matter. It wouldn't stick any more than going to Detox did this time or the time before or the time before that.

This was the dark side, he thought, sitting here with a stranger in bed full of your sperm, waiting for morning and not even knowing when it will come.

He looked for the bottle he remembered buying at Harry's just before they left—a fifth of cheap rye. He couldn't remember drinking it. He searched everywhere and finally found it in the flap pocket of his jacket. He held it up to the dim light of the window and saw that he hadn't even cracked the seal. He cut the paper with his thumbnail and unscrewed the cap and drank as much as he could without breathing and without having it dribble back out of his nose. It surged down his throat like a wall of fire. He wiped his mouth with the back of his hand and drank some more and sat there and waited, feeling like Lazarus in hell, waiting for morning.

When the glow started and the door to the cage suddenly opened and his demon stepped out, he felt like crowing he was feeling so good. He was like a whole different person. He had this new kind of flame at the center of his being that felt like courage or steadfastness—a wild fire loose in his blood surging all over. Whatever the boy lost yesterday and whatever Homer lost whenever he lost it, so long ago he couldn't remember, the whiskey gave it back to him increased tenfold. He was so grateful, he drank some more whiskey and then kept on drinking until he fell asleep at the table.

LATER THAT MORNING, the sun spilled into the room. The woman woke and shuddered and got dressed and left without even washing her face or combing her hair or putting on lipstick. By the time Homer finally woke up the morning had passed and the sun had already started declining. He did not know where he was for a moment. Then he remembered the woman. He looked at the bed—she wasn't there. He remembered the bottle. He picked it up from the floor—it was empty. Either he had drunk it all, or he passed out before he was through and she finished it off. His head hurt, and his stomach was upset, and he seemed to have pissed on the floor. It was all wet underneath the chair. Unless it was whiskey.

He tried to get up and abruptly sat back down and waited a while. He tried again and walked carefully to the sink and washed his face. He saw his trousers near the door and picked them up. His wallet was gone. It didn't much matter. He figured he already spent all the money. Then he checked the mattress and couldn't believe it. The money in the slit was gone. Everything he had in the world was gone. He sat in the chair and stared at the blank wash of light in the window and wondered about it. He wondered how a man could lose so much over and over and over again and still not be dead and still seem to have more to lose even after he lost it all.

- EIGHT -

AFTER THEY DROPPED Homer off at the courthouse,
the boy and his daddy headed back home. As
soon as they cleared the woods and drove up to the
front of the house, his momma came rushing out of
the door as though she was attached to the truck with
a spring. It hadn't even quit rolling good when she was
already running along beside it, trying to open the
door. The boy didn't know if she was trying to climb
in or pull him out instead.

When she got the door open, it was neither one. She
stuck her head in and tried to kiss him. The boy reared
back, and she hugged his legs.

"You all right?" she said. "You do all right?"

She looked at her husband.

"He do all right, Jake? How did he do?"

"He did all right," his daddy said, getting out of the
driver's seat.

"Let me out," the boy said, pushing his momma back with his hands, trying to get her to let loose of his legs.

He didn't want to have to sit there with his daddy gone and her hanging on him, blocking the way. Besides that, his daddy was lying. He did it all wrong.

"Tell me about it," his momma said, smiling at him, acting like she was happy to see him.

"Let me out."

"Leave him alone," his daddy said. "He lost his cock."

"Lost it?"

She acted as though he misplaced it somewhere. How could he lose it?

"It was killed. Leave him alone now, and go get us some supper. We're mighty hungry. Ain't that right?" he asked the boy.

"Yes, sir."

The boy climbed up in the rear of the truck and started unloading the cages. He didn't want to talk about it.

"Fighting like that makes you hungry," his daddy said. "Come on, Lily. Leave him alone. Let him unpack and do the chores. He's got all those chickens to tend to, and I got a few beers waiting, I reckon."

"I'll help him a minute," his momma said.

"He don't need it. He knows what to do. Come on in the house."

The boy didn't look at them when they left. He never knew he would be so ashamed. She was his momma. He shouldn't have minded, but he was ashamed anyway.

He took the cocks back to their cages. The Claret looked sick. It seemed to the boy it might not make it. He checked its head. It wasn't white. He reminded himself to tell his daddy. Then he washed out the carrying cases and set them in the storehouse to dry. He put the medicine back on the shelves and wrapped the case of gaffs in the old towel his daddy kept it in so it wouldn't get dusty. The towel was lightly oiled with twenty-weight motor oil to keep the leather from drying out, except his momma said it wasn't leather. It was just Naugahyde, and the hides of naugas don't dry out because they ain't real leather.

But his daddy said he was going to do it anyway, the same way he did everything else he wanted. What was the sense in having a boy if he didn't do what he wanted him to?

No sense, I reckon, his momma said.

Then shut up about it, and let me do it, his daddy said. It ain't your business. And he told the boy to keep that towel oiled. He didn't want those gaffs rusting on him and the case getting dirty.

After the boy finished unloading, he fed and watered the other cocks, and all the while he never looked at the empty cage. He knew it was there, but he never even looked at it.

AFTER SUPPER they watched TV. It was a Western with John Wayne in it, and his daddy said there wasn't anything he liked better than that except a good Clint Eastwood movie.

His momma said, "There aren't any good Clint Eastwood movies."

She didn't like John Wayne or Clint Eastwood movies, and the only reason she watched them, she said, was the TV just had one channel at a time, and they already had it on.

"Damn right it's on," his daddy said.

He settled down to some serious beer drinking. It was Saturday night, and that was when he usually started, unless he started Saturday morning. The rest of the week he was at work, except for Sunday, and he didn't drink on Sunday out of respect for the Lord.

That's the only way you respect Him, his momma said.

And his daddy said, You don't know, Lily. You can't see my heart.

And his momma said, That's right. You're right. I reckon I better hush up about it. I can't say a thing about your heart except to mention how black it is, and the good Lord knows that already. That's the only reason I'm not saying something about it.

And his daddy laughed and said, If that isn't saying something about it, Lily, I'd sure hate to hear it when you are.

AFTER THE MOVIE, the boy went to bed. His momma and daddy were still sitting up, and he heard them talking.

"Tell me about it," his momma said.

"Nothing to tell."

"You know what I mean. Tell me what happened."

His daddy told about the first three cocks and Homer's betting.

"How'd he do?" his momma asked.

"He did all right. You know Homer. I didn't trust him."

"Why not?"

"Why not? You know why not. If there's any way to cheat on something, Homer'll do it. He doesn't have an honest bone in his body."

"He had a hard time," his momma said.

"Don't give me that, Lily. I had a hard time. You had a hard time. We all had a hard time. That's how it is. As long as you're alive, you're going to have a hard time. The only time you're not is when you're dead, and he's working on that. He's working on that every chance he got. You know what he did? He bet on his own hook. I mean, outside of what I gave him. He bet against me and changed the odds and knocked down, I reckon, a hundred, a hundred and fifty dollars, and then claimed he was broke and wanted me to give him some."

"You do it?"

"Yeah. I don't know why I did, but I did."

"You knew that I would if you didn't."

"That's right."

"You're a good man, Jake."

His daddy laughed.

"I mean, in some things," she said. "Don't get too big-headed about it."

He laughed again.

"I won't. Not with you here to remind me, I won't. I just didn't want him pestering you."

"He doesn't pester me."

"Pestering *me,* then."

THEN THEY WERE QUIET, and the boy looked up at the window beside him. The night was dark, and he could see the stars along the line of trees on the mountain.

Seeing the stars made him feel lonely—they were so few and the rest of the sky was so big and dark. When he was little, his momma told him the stars were the souls of the dearly departed, shining in the dark, and when he asked her what that meant, she said the stars were the souls of their loved ones—all the dead dearly departed like Mamaw and Pawpaw and all the others dead and gone before. He didn't know they had as many dearly departed as that. There were just a few he could think of, and there were more stars than he could count, but he didn't say anything about it. He didn't believe her anyway. The stars were cold, and some of them were burned out already. It just took a while for light to get here. He heard about it on TV. As far as he knew, most of them were burned out already. We just didn't know it yet. He imagined the whole sky dark as a blanket. That's what bothered him about it. Maybe that's why he felt so lonely. It was too dark, and the stars were too small, and the spaces between them were too immense. The moon hadn't even come out yet, and when it did, it wouldn't help. Nothing would help. It would still be dark. The light of the moon was a dark, dark light. Everything looked like negatives in it.

His momma and daddy started talking again. They were murmuring like bees in the wall, and the boy could hardly tell at first if he was really hearing them or if he was just making it up. It didn't sound like it was coming from the other room. It sounded like it was inside his head. The words were different, but it was the same sort of thing he'd been saying back and forth to himself all day long, ever since it happened. He'd thought of it as all one thing ever since he had left home that morning. But he knew it wasn't. It was one certain, specific event that he still hadn't figured out, and if he could just get a hold of that, the whole thing would come together, and he would finally be free of it. He listened thinking that maybe now the last piece would fall into place, and the door would spring open, or the pieces would all come together, and he would be whole once again. It was as though he was the puzzle, and something had happened. He had all the pieces, but he hadn't been able to get them all back together again because the old way didn't work. The puzzle had changed. It had rearranged itself. That was the hard thing to figure about it. All the parts were the same as they'd always been, but they didn't seem to fit anymore. The puzzle was different. He was going to have to figure it out all over again. The buzzing he heard was the sound of his own mind, the pulleys and weights and gears in his brain, buzzing around, working on it. The picture he saw was that of a large, mainframe computer with orange disks like those on TV, whirling around, going one way, then reversing themselves and going the other, emitting a buzzing noise as they went back and forth, trying to figure out the problem. The name of the disks was the same name as the mainframe itself. It was called *Orange Crush* after the color of the disks, which were named for the hat he wore with his daddy. None of it made any sense, but that's how it was. That was another part of the puzzle.

THEN ALL OF A SUDDEN the whole thing fell into place and locked in as soon as he heard his momma say, "What happened then?"

"Little shit blew it."

"It wasn't his fault."

"The hell it wasn't. Whose fault was it?"

"He was too young."

"You mean it's my fault."

"I didn't say that. I'm not talking about fault."

"I am."

"I told you. He's just a boy. You shouldn't have trusted him."

"I didn't trust him. I didn't trust him any more than I trusted that brother of yours. Neither one of them got any sense. I got to do all their thinking for them, and that wears me out. I get tired sometimes."

"I know you do."

"I get tired, Lily. It wears me out, and I get discouraged. I'm discouraged right now."

"I know you are. We're all discouraged. Who wouldn't be, considering what happened?"

"All that money."

"That isn't important."

"It isn't to you. It is to me."

"I'm thinking about Sonny."

"He's all right. He's just a boy."

"That's what I mean."

"That's right. I thought it was time to start him on cocks, but I was wrong. He's too young for that."

"You put too big a burden on him. He wasn't ready."

"Damn right he wasn't ready. He didn't do shit."

"You got to train him."

"That's what I'm doing."

"And not get discouraged. Getting discouraged isn't going to help."

"Neither is losing that cock. That was the best cock I ever saw. I don't mean the best one I raised. I mean the best one I ever saw. If they had a hall of fame for cocks, that would be the first one they'd want to let in it."

"You said it wasn't Sonny's fault."

"It was, and it wasn't. I thought he couldn't lose with that cock, and he did."

"You said it had some kind of disease."

"It did, but he should have told me about it."

"He didn't know."

"I know he didn't."

"He's just a boy. Let him stay here with me next time."

"Damn right. I wouldn't take him."

"Let him feed the birds and clean out their cages. That way he won't have to know about it, you not taking him next time."

"One thing I hate is that he didn't tell me. He just threw that cock away."

"I don't see how he could have known."

"I'd have known," his daddy said. "If it was me, I would have told."

"That's silly, Jake. You don't know what you'd do if you were him."

"I'd have taken an interest in it. You know me. I'd do it like I do right now. I always have and I always will."

"I know that, Jake."

"I'm not like him. Never have been and never will be."

As soon as the boy heard his daddy say that, the last piece snapped into place. He wasn't his daddy and never would be, and not only that, he never would even want to be. Each one was different. That was the puzzle.

They went on talking some more, but he wasn't listening. He was through with that. He was thinking about Lion. The moon had come up over Snake Nation Mountain and filled the room with its radiant light. Black was white and white was black, as though the whole world had been transformed into a roll of negative film. There were no colors. To get it straight you had to turn the whole thing around backward.

He thought about Lion's cage out there empty and the other cocks without any names sitting on their perches asleep, and he knew there was nothing out there anymore, nothing he would want to get up and go to. He would wake in the morning, and his daddy would tell him to feed the cocks, and he wouldn't do it. His daddy would ask him why, and he wouldn't tell him, and his daddy would say because he was afraid, that's why. Just because he went out the first time and lost his cock didn't mean he was going to do it the next time. He was too young, that's all. He'd just wait a year or two, and then he'd be ready. You get knocked down or fall off something, you don't just lie there. You get up and do it again and keep on doing it till sooner or later you beat the son of a bitch, he'd say. That's how you do.

But it wasn't that. It wasn't about winning or losing or trying again. It was about grabbing Lion by the head and slinging him around in a circle and throwing him underhand into the corner. That's when it happened—whatever his daddy wanted to teach him about winning and losing and falling off and getting up and being a man. It wasn't the white head or the man from Tennessee gaffing Lion worse than the cock Lion was fighting. It wasn't even Lion's dying on him the first time he did it. It was having to kill him again, and doing it, and not only that, being willing to do it. That's what he didn't understand.

It took all that time and all that thinking to figure it out, and it wasn't what his daddy thought. He thought it was about money and winning and losing and learning how to be like him. But if that's what it was to be like his daddy, he didn't want it. He'd just as soon be like Homer. But he wasn't Homer either. He wasn't his daddy, and he wasn't Homer. He wasn't anything but himself. That's what he always was, as long back as he could remember, and that's what he was going to be for the rest of his life. Killing that cock was like killing himself—like killing all his daddy's hopes and aspirations for him—and what was left over after he did it was what he was now. It's like something broke or tore loose, and he came out—like all the cages around him had opened.

AFTER A WHILE he fell asleep. Toward morning he had a dream, and in his dream the cages all opened, and Lion came to the edge and looked out, and he realized suddenly that the cock wasn't dead. He hadn't killed him. His heart leaped up as soon as he saw him. But it wasn't Lion. That was the funny thing about it. It looked like Lion, but it wasn't Lion. It was himself. He was the one at the edge of the cage.

Some time after that, something woke him—a night bird or a rooster crowing—and he got up out of bed and went to the window. The moon was setting over Snake Nation Mountain. He looked out at the light and at the whole world turned around backward and wondered if it would ever get straight again. The world suddenly seemed strange to him, like a whole new place, the way it did first thing in the morning after a deep snow. He didn't know if he would ever get used to it.

Just then a cock started crowing. Then another. Then all of them were crowing together. It sounded like a hundred broken engines at once trying to get started on a cold morning. But that's not the sound he heard. What he heard were angels singing one after another in rounds, singing an old song his momma taught him.

Row, row, row, your boat, the first cock crowed.

Then another.

Then another, coming in on that.

Pretty soon they were all singing together.

Merrily, merrily, merrily, merrily, they all crowed in confusion, *Life is but a dream.*

And he suddenly realized that it was not night. It was the next morning.

HE CREPT over to the other side of the bed and picked up his shoes and the pile of loose clothes he'd thrown over there the night before. He tiptoed to the door and turned the knob slowly so it wouldn't rattle, then he eased on down the hall and opened the front door. The cold took his breath away, it was so sharp. Then he controlled it. He closed the door slowly behind him, easing it shut until he heard it click. He went down the steps and walked out on the white pad of the gravel. The pale silver moon was fading, but the sun hadn't come up yet. It was as though the air was lit. Or the gravel. Each thing held its own light. That's how he could see what it was.

When he got far enough away from the house, he paused for a minute and put on his clothes. Then he went straight to the line of cages. The first one he came to was empty. He went on past it and came to the second and looked in and saw the beady eye looking at him. It was like a seed of light, and he thought to himself, That's what makes them crow in the morning. They got that seed of light in them. God made them like that the same way he made them courageous and steadfast.

The cock turned away and rubbed its beak on the side of the perch. It was a Claret, the ruff bright red and amber in the light. He opened the door to the cage, and the cock quit rubbing the side of its beak and tried to back off as he reached for it. He got his hand under the cock in a handle, his whole palm between its legs. He felt the stiff grain of the feathers and lifted him out. The cock tried to pull away, but he clapped his other hand on its wings and pulled it against his chest and held it there for a minute the same way he used to hold Lion. Then he took his hand, put it on the cock's neck, and jerked it around one quick turn—then another—and let go. The bird went spinning, pinwheeling in the dust and dirt of the yard, bouncing off the legs of the cages, ramming up against a tree, sliding off and running around over and over on top of itself, kicking up dust that drifted in the early morning sun that was just coming down in shafts through the tops of the pines on the edge of the woods. He thought of the wheels on the throne of God his momma told him about in the Bible, made out of angel heads that were spinning. It was all eyes. The whole throne of God was made of eyes spinning like that. Then it was quiet.

The dust drifted and turned to gold and fell from the air, and he went to the next cage and took out a Butcher and killed it the same way. Then he went faster. He didn't even take time to watch. He could hear them flapping behind him, but he didn't look. He just saw the dust that was drifting like gold dust in the air.

Then he was through. The last cage was empty now, just like the first one that had held Lion. He turned, and a couple of the birds were still going like dogs that had been poisoned. Then it was quiet, and he saw the sunlight and knew it was morning. The dust of the ruckus drifted past him, and he couldn't tell the grains of the light from the grains of dust that were falling through it. It was all golden. The morning was full of golden light. He never knew that about it before. He had never seen it look like that, not in that particular way. Everything was kind of ordinary. It was just like a regular, ordinary day, except it wasn't. It was all brand-new.

The whole world was brand-new.

Then he went and picked up the chickens and piled them on top of each other. He thought he might burn them, but he was too tired. He thought about going back to bed he was so tired, but it was too late for that. It felt like he had a seed growing in him. He wasn't finished. That's what it felt like. It felt like something else that was coming.

HIS MOMMA was already in the kitchen, fussing around with some plants in the window. They were mostly all cactus. Some bloomed a little every spring and some in the winter around Christmas. His momma said they were just like her. They got by on nothing. That's why she loved them.

"Where you been?" his momma asked.

"Out."

"Doing what?"

"Messing around."

"Messing around with those chickens."

The boy grunted just like his daddy and opened the refrigerator and got out some milk and drank one glassful and then another.

"Leave some for your daddy."

"There's some."

The boy poured another glass.

"You hear what I said?"

The boy didn't answer. He drank the milk.

"Hear what?" his daddy said, coming in the room with his shoes in his hand and his socks on his feet. One of the socks had a hole in the toe, and he pulled it off and put it on the other foot so his big toe wouldn't stick out the front.

"Cut your toenails, you wouldn't have a hole in your sock," his momma said.

"Keep up with the mending, I wouldn't either."

He put on his shoes and grunted as he bent to tie the laces.

The boy thought he sounded like a pig. He grunted back at him.

His daddy looked up.

"What?"

The boy didn't answer.

"What's that?"

The boy didn't know. Something was happening. Something was happening inside in his chest, filling him up.

He grunted again.

His daddy got up.

"What the hell you think you're doing? You making fun of me or what?"

He broke off.

"What the hell's he doing, Lily?"

"I don't know."

She looked alarmed.

He turned to the boy.

"You do the birds?"

He nodded his head yes. He did the birds.

It was a joke.

He grunted again and started laughing.

"Talk to me, you little shit. You water them?"

The boy looked at him and shook his head no.

"You feed them?"

The boy shook his head no.

"You clean the cages?"

He shook his head no.

He could see his daddy clenching his fist.

"You didn't feed them. You didn't water them. How the hell you do them, then?"

The boy looked at him and opened his mouth, but it wasn't a mouth. It was too hard for a mouth. It was more like a beak. And it wasn't words. It was a roaring. The words came out in a whirling of eyes and a roaring like the roar of a lion. And he remembered what Homer said.

The cock and the lion are the only animals God ever made that are courageous and steadfast, he remembered telling Homer.

Except for a man, Homer said. Except for a man.

FRANK MANLEY is the Charles Howard Candler Professor of Renaissance Literature and Director of the Creative Writing Program at Emory University. His other works include *Within the Ribbons: 9 Stories* and *Resultances,* winner of the Devins Award for Poetry. Manley's writing has been included in *The Best of a Decade: New Stories from the South.*